ᶠᵒʳᶜ

THE WINDSOR SECRET

Books by **David Cullen**

The Eye of Makarios
The Mesrine Conclusion
The Windsor Secret
Pick Up Sticks
Knock On My Door
The Baalbeck Decision

THE WINDSOR SECRET

Ω

DAVID CULLEN

Culpro Books

The Windsor Secret
First published 2005
Revised and updated International Edition 2009

ISBN: 978-0-9559911-2-7

www.lulu.com/davidcullen

Published Culpro Books
an imprint of Cullen Productions

"Anyone who knows the secret, dies. That's the point, don't you see?"
- Ron Becker,
Friday August 29 1997

Ω

Revenge is a dish...

For Will – never forgotten.
And for the real Claudette and Gisele.

Ω

Cast in order of appearance

Prince Charles *(ex-husband and heir to the throne of Britain)*
Diana, Princess of Wales *(ex-wife, and mother of the future King of England)*
Sarah *(Duchess of York)*
Billy *(a butler)*
Her Majesty Queen Elizabeth the Queen Mother *(keeper of a secret)*
Ilich Ramirov *(The Contractor)*
Wallis Simpson Windsor *(Duchess of Windsor and erstwhile keeper of a secret)*
Sir Kenneth Dean *(The Catalyst)*
Christina Cascianis *(Israeli Intelligence (and still a special lady))*
Stelios Grivas *(a ghost)*
A Daughter *(seeking knowledge and revenge)*
Will The Cat *(a companion)*
Eric Dejeune *(a prison officer)*
Chaim Cohen *(Israeli Intelligence – and a Catholic priest)*
Dr Daniel Salinger *(Medical examiner)*
Teresa Cotton *(assistant to Christina Cascianis)*
Melanie Nathanson *(Israeli Intelligence)*
Barking Dog *(no point in having one and barking yourself)*
Charles Fleury-Goujon *(Commissaire of Police, BCP Paris (retired))*
Pierre Jamo *(Chief Inspector of Police, BCP Paris)*
Maurice Goise *(Sergeant of Police, BCP Paris)*
Claudette Ibrahim *(Inspector of Police, BCP Paris)*
The Secretary to Her Majesty Queen Elizabeth the Queen

Mother

The Medical Consultant to Her Majesty Queen Elizabeth the Queen Mother

Ron Becker *(The Rag, British Embassy Paris)*

Gisele Joudeh *(a Lebanese diplomat)*

The Professor *(scary)*

John Smith *(Head of Charles' People)*

Camilla *(future Queen of England)*

Veronique Chevalier *(a socialite)*

Michel Chevalier *(husband and lawyer)*

Henri *(owner of the best bar in Paris)*

Gillian Colet *(Commissaire of Police, BCP Paris)*

Eli Lucas *(a journalist)*

Claude Dumoulin *(a paparazzo (one of many))*

Jack Jones *(Head of Betty's Men)*

Madame Renée/Sylvie Jacquot *(still in love)*

LouLou *(a tart, no matter which sex)*

Concierge of 1 Rue Lamarck, Paris

Receptionist at the British Embassy, Paris

Concierge of The Ritz Hotel, Paris

Assistant Director of Security, Ritz Hotel, Paris

Henri Paul *(acting Director of Security, Ritz Hotel, Paris)*

Emad 'Dodi' Fayed *(in the wrong place at the wrong time)*

Her Majesty Queen Elizabeth II of England

Ω

FOREWORD

It was Lord Byron who said, "Truth is always strange; stranger than fiction." But why is it that we humans will readily accept fiction but always disbelieve the truth if it stretches beyond our own narrow perception of what truth is?

Truth is not history. And history is not truth. History is written by the winners, by those who survive to tell the tale (and who want, perhaps, to justify their actions). The real truth is often what the victors do not want us to hear.

And, unlike in fiction, life is not just three characters. Life is not just the hero, the villain, the girl or the guy. Life is a mêlée of people whose paths criss-cross with one another. Each day of our lives we cross the paths of hundreds, sometimes thousands, of people, lives touching, different people with different aims all coming together.

The previous stories – *The Eye of Makarios* and *The Mesrine Conclusion* – were unconnected. *The Windsor Secret* is a natural follow-on from both of them – but nevertheless it stands on its own, an alternative recording of historical fact.

Where does fiction end and truth begin? As Voltaire said:

"On doit des égards aux vivants; on ne doit aux morts que la vérité."

– We owe respect to the living; to the dead we owe *only* truth.

David Cullen

Ω

PROLOGUE

Christmas 1986
Sandringham, Norfolk, England

"You are a whore!" The raised voice coming from behind the closed door of the west-facing bedroom on the first floor was unmistakeable. A famous voice, an often-imitated voice, and identical to the voice of his mentor and idol Louis Mountbatten.

When the voice spoke in a normal, unstressed tone it was regal and refined. But nowadays it seemed to be raised constantly, always shouting, at least when his wife was about.

The servants going about their business in this, the Norfolk country home of the Sovereign, had heard it all before.

The couple had been married for five years, a marriage of convenience, the future King of England and the non-Catholic virgin with a lineage going back to King Charles I, chosen as a brood mare by his real – but sadly already married – lover.

There had never been love ("Whatever that is"), not from his side. As for her, she had convinced herself that this was the real thing, the true love of fairy tales, the Princess Bride. But even before the marriage – witnessed by the world five and a half years previously on July 29 1981 – she knew she was deluding herself. He had had many sexual partners, including her own sister, but she knew that he had love for only one woman – and that woman was not her.

By the time she stood on the steps of St Paul's Cathedral and watched the world cheering, she knew that she would never be Queen.

Dutifully she had born the children. The future King, William Arthur Philip Louis (how she hated those last two names!) on June 21 1982, and the surviving twin Henry Charles Albert David on September 15 1984. Perhaps it was because the other twin, the girl, had been stillborn that his hatred of her grew in intensity – he had so wanted a daughter. Or perhaps it was because he suspected that the twins were not his ("Look at the red hair. He looks just like him!").

But now he had somehow found out about Barry. It was stupid of her to think that she could get away with it, she knew she was watched everywhere – but she had needed someone to listen to her, someone to understand her, someone to be kind to her… Someone to love her, even if only physically.

"Oh, a whore am I?" she retaliated. "I have had two men ever in my life. *Two!* If I am a whore, what does that make *you?* The man who sleeps with whomever he chooses? The man who has his mistress installed in the same house as his wife and children– "

"Oh do shut up."

"What's good for you is good for me. I am not having a marriage of three people."

"What do you mean? You are being hysterical. I am the future King of England - "

"You are a man. You are not divine. *You are my husband.* Tell me you are not fucking her."

"Do you really expect me to be the only Prince of Wales who never had a mistress?"

"*What?* So you are not denying it - "

"We are talking about *you*. You have been screwing your bodyguard – I have proof."

"Proof? Proof! What do you have? Tell me! Show me."

"I do not need to. Just tell me, how *could* you?"

"How *could* I? This coming from the man, the family, that is the coldest on earth. How could you ever understand, you're all automatons."

"So you are not denying it."

"You just prove it."

"I don't have to prove it. Why do you think he was transferred? I have had my suspicions for months - "

"Kind of you to even notice me."

" – but you have still been seeing him."

"Prove it."

"Well, you will never see him again."

There was a pause. Her voice was lower, calmer, as she asked, "Charles, what have you done?"

Quietness. Then Charles said, "I have resolved the problem. Commensurate with the threat posed."

"Threat?" Diana shook her head in disbelief. "What threat is he to you?"

"You do know that it is treason to screw the King's wife, don't you?"

"What are you talking about?"

"And you know the penalty for treason."

There was a smash, the breaking of glass. The bedroom door flew open and Diana ran out.

Sarah, the new vivacious, red-headed Duchess of York, was coming along the corridor. "Di?" she asked as she saw her friend running towards her. "Darling, are you okay?"

Diana stopped in front of her, tears streaming down her face. "Oh, Fergie," she hugged her friend. "I can't stand it, I just can't stand it."

Sarah held up the bottle she was carrying. "Come up to my room, tell me about it. Let's have some wine. Andrew is still downstairs."

"No. No, I want to see Grandma. Is she still downstairs?"

"She came up about half an hour ago. Had a few."

"I must see her." Diana turned and ran back towards the southern end of the building.

Ω

Billy the butler was just coming out of the room as Diana hurried down the corridor.

"Billy! Is Grandma awake?"

"Her Majesty is reading, your Highness." The butler closed the door behind him.

"I must see her."

"I would rather she wasn't disturbed. I have just put her down for the night. She has, er, celebrated the season a little too vigorously."

Diana tapped on the door. "You mean she's pissed."

"Your Highness, I hardly think - "

But Diana had entered the room, purposefully closing the door behind her in the butler's face.

By royal bedroom standards the room was quite small but it was plushly decorated, reflecting the Jacobean style of the downstairs rooms.

The large bed was against the wall on the left, positioned so that the old lady – who preferred to sleep on her left side – had a view through the window and out over the west lawns when she woke in the mornings.

An antique brass bedside lamp cast a pool of diffused light over the bed and created an opulent penumbra over the rest of the room.

The eighty-six year old matriarch of the British Royal Family lay propped up in bed, pince-nez reading glasses on the end of her nose, *The Times* open on her lap. Her open mouth and closed eyes indicated that the affairs of the world were temporarily in suspension.

On the bedside cabinet stood a nearly-empty glass containing a centimetre of colourless liquid.

"Grandma?" Diana walked across the red patterned Persian carpet. "Grandma!"

The old woman's left arm jumped and she opened her eyes. For a moment she was confused, then her face softened when she looked at her caller.

"Grandma?" repeated Diana.

The old woman smiled. "I'm sorry my darling," there was genuine affection in her voice for her granddaughter-in-law. "I must have dozed off. I told Billy to go."

"Oh Grandma, I don't think I can stand it." Diana sat down on the edge of the bed.

"What is it dear? Is he being beastly again?"

"You don't know the half of it. That bitch is behind it, I know she is. He is always accusing me of things – "

"Does he still think Harry is not his?"

"Oh, he denies ever having said that. But it's still there. I can see it every time he looks at him. He never holds him, you know."

"Men are strange creatures, Diana. And there are none more strange than the men in this family. I have done my best, but they can be so cold, so unemotional. Even more than their position obviously requires. His father's genes don't help, of course. Here, take this will you?" The old lady closed the newspaper and moved it towards Diana. As Diana took it off the bed and folded it up, the old lady reached across for her glass. "Is the bottle there?"

Diana opened the door of the bedside cabinet, placed the newspaper inside and removed the familiar green glass bottle. "I don't think there's any tonic."

"Doesn't matter. A strong one will help me sleep."

Diana unscrewed the lid and poured the clear liquid into the proffered glass.

"You really must try not to let him antagonise you," counselled the old lady as she raised the glass and drank. "Until your marriage he was always the centre of attention. Now you have taken that away from him - "

"Its not my fault."

"I never said it was, my dear. But nevertheless, you have taken away his spotlight. You are a married couple, a prince and his princess, the future King and Queen. And yet the world craves only you."

"Loved by the world yet despised by my husband!" Diana put the bottle back in the cabinet and closed the door.

"He sees himself as a bit-player. He is not used to it – and, dare I say, he is not yet mature enough to cope. That's why he still consoles himself with his friend."

"But what about me?"

The old lady took another large mouthful of drink. "You were told it would not be easy. That he would not be easy."

"I know, Grandma, I know. But I was in love with him. Or at least I fooled myself into thinking that I was."

"And now?"

"Now?"

"Are you in love with him?"

Diana sighed. "He is my husband, of course I am. But the question is, is he in love with me?"

"You would be surprised. He loves you, in his own way."

"Well, he has a very funny way. Coldness and accusations, that's all I get from him. Do you know we haven't had sex since Harry was conceived?"

The old lady's eyebrows rose as she emptied her glass. In the last few minutes she had drunk two hundred millilitres of neat gin. She said, "He will come round eventually you know. He will acknowledge Henry as his, when he starts to grow and look like him."

Diana took the glass from her. She did not comment directly but she said, "It's not that this time."

"What is it? The twin again?"

"No, this time it is something different." Diana took the pince-nez off the old lady's nose and put them on the cabinet. "Do you remember Barry, my previous bodyguard? He was moved onto other duties just before Andrew and Fer – Sarah's wedding last July?"

"Not really, dear, no."

"Well, now Charles is accusing me of sleeping with him. Of having an affair."

The old lady closed her eyes.

"And," continued Diana, "he is threatening to do something awful to him."

Slowly, the old lady's eyelids re-opened.

"And did you?"

"What?"

"Have an affair with him?"

"An affair? No."

"Thank goodness. One should confine oneself to affairs with one's own class. So what is he threatening to do? Nothing rash, I hope."

Diana shrugged. "You know him. He might find it difficult to make up his mind on most things, but when he does…"

"Well we can't have that, c-can we?" The old lady's speech was now distinctly slurring. "The man has been moved on, he should now be left alone. Royalty is no place for vendettas." To her dying day she never realised the hypocrisy in those words. "We… we must get him to lay off. We all have our skeletons, our little s-s-secrets. Even I do." She nodded, speaking to herself. "Good heavens, if his Grandfather had ever known! But he never did find out. Thank goodness. That was so, so long ago now."

Diana giggled lovingly. "You have a secret, Grandma?"

The old lady suddenly looked at her sternly, and the smile dropped from Diana's face. "Oh yes, I have a secret. A secret that can never be told. People have died to protect it." Her eyes clouded as she thought back over the years. "Too many people. Anyone who knows it has been killed. To my sh-shame I have even used it as an excuse for my own revenge. As if the secret wasn't horrible enough. If… they ever… found out… " She closed her eyes again and her breathing became deeper.

"Grandma?" Diana shook her shoulder. "Grandma?"

"Mm?" Half of one eye opened.

"Grandma," asked Diana. "What is this secret?"

[Police Sergeant Barry Mannakee was killed in a road accident in East London on May 15 1987.]

8 months earlier...

Thursday April 24 1986
Boulevard Suchet, Paris, France

At 02:00 in the morning the streets of the 16th Arrondisement in Paris are still and almost deserted. Occasionally a taxi might cruise past carrying home a resident of this most exclusive quarter of the French capital. Here and there a solitary figure may be walking, having missed the last metro. Once or twice a week revelry may be heard from within one or other of the fashionable residences, an all-night party which the givers could not afford but had to hold for appearances' sake; for even in this day and age, appearances among the super, nouveau or manqué rich were everything.

But the streets did not matter to the man now moving slowly but purposefully over the rooftops. He was dressed in a black combat outfit and black balaclava hood. The apartment blocks on the east side of the street were taller than the houses on this side, and that was an irritation. There were a few lights on in the apartments but if anyone was looking out they were unlikely to see him, such was his skill. But nevertheless he glanced up occasionally at the windows; if he saw anyone looking out, he would silence them later.

His face was still boyish at thirty-seven years of age, still belying the powerful body underneath it. The hair was longer nowadays, but it was still wavy and pushed back. Its natural colour was black, but underneath the balaclava it was currently dyed blond. He no longer wore the tinted, plain glass spectacles which he was wearing in that full face photo that always appeared in the Press whenever his name was mentioned – a photo which was now nearly fifteen years old. He had not worn the spectacles since he had lost his right eye in Amsterdam twelve years previously. But judicious use of contact lenses ensured that not only was his sensitive left eye shielded from irritating daylight but also that no one knew that he was half blind – not even the doctors that used to give him his six-monthly medicals in Moscow before he was cast off by his masters as not needed anymore.

Not that 'half blind' meant the same for him as it did for normal people. For this man had been trained from an early age. The Russian state had taken him into care at the age of eleven, and he had been subject to seven years of the most intense and specialised training to augment and enhance his already natural ability to kill things in the most inventive – and sometimes painful – ways. The use of one eye to this man was the same as the use of four eyes to normal men.

He reached the building he wanted. From around his waist he unwound the thin but incredibly strong micro-fibre rope and looped one end around the chimney stack. The other end he threw over the side of the building.

One tug on the rope to ensure it was secured, and then Ilich Ramirov lowered himself smoothly over the side of number 24 Boulevard Suchet…

Bessie Wallis Warfield Spencer Simpson Windsor lay flat on her back in the centre of the wide double-bed under the crisp white sheet and maroon and gold filigreed eiderdown. Her black painted hair was spread out roughly on the bolster. Her mouth was hanging open, but after three facelifts that had tightened her throat so much that she could swallow nothing exceeding one centimetre in width, her airways were too tight to permit any snoring. Her head was propped up by four pillows so that she was permanently in a semi-upright position, so that she could breathe. She looked like a queen lying in state – something history had decreed she would never be.

She was just a few weeks off of her ninetieth birthday (on June 19), and to many it was a surprise not only how she had lived to such a vast age but that she had survived at all after the death of her husband fourteen years previously. "Sheer bloody-mindedness," her arch enemy – and, tonight, her nemesis – in London had called it.

Ilich Ramirov stood by the bed, looking down at her. He had no time for consideration or sentiment, a contract was a contract and he had been paid very handsomely. But this was his first British royal – or, he corrected himself, non-royal. The Duchess of Windsor she may be, but fifty years ago it had been decreed that she was never ever to be royal.

He heard a sound from outside the bedroom door. He froze. As he heard the doorknob turning he took one step backwards into the lee of the ornate, solid-wood wardrobe.

A sharp, wedge-shaped crack of light penetrated the darkness of the room as the night nurse peeked in. She came over to the bed and tucked in the sheet and smoothed down a strand of the Duchess' hair. Quietly she went out again, never knowing that Death was standing just two metres away.

As the wedge of light vanished, Ramirov moved back out and over to the bed. They had told him to make it look natural – and those that paid the piper called the tune. He leant forward and with the gentleness of a parent holding a newborn baby he put his left arm around the Duchess' head and lifted her forwards. With his right hand he pulled away all four pillows and let them fall to the floor. Carefully he began to lower her back down.

Suddenly her eyes sprang open. She stared straight at Ramirov. He looked at her and stopped lowering.

Her mouth moved. The sound came out moments later, like an out-of-sync movie. "David? David, is that you?"

He said nothing.

"*David?*"

"Yes, Peaches." He knew that that was her husband's pet name for her. "It is me." He felt the bony neck in his hand relax.

"Oh, it – it has been so long. I thought you would never come back for me. You do still love me, don't you David?"

"Of course, my darling," he spoke softly. "You have always been the woman I love."

"Oh, David! My beautiful little man - "

Slowly he began to lower her again.

"Kiss me," she said. "Kiss me and tell me it will be all right."

He bent forward and put his lips on hers. Her perfume almost covered the rankness of her breath from all the medicines in her body. "It will be all right, Peaches."

"I love you, my David."

Her head touched the mattress and he removed his hand.

It took one minute and sixteen seconds for her to stop breathing.

Ramirov waited for fifteen minutes after her heart stopped beating before he lifted the head back upright and replaced the four pillows. She would be found later, a natural death.

By the time Ramirov had his leg over the windowsill, microrope in his hand, her spirit had left her body. He felt no other presence in the room, just a slight odour where the cadaver had vacated itself.

He looked over to the bed and said, "Welcome to history, bitch."

Faubourg St Honoré, Paris, France

At 03:28 the telephone rang in the plush office on the first floor of the British Embassy on Faubourg St Honoré. Normally nighttime calls would be taken by the Night Duty Officer in the MI6 room downstairs, but this extension had deliberately not been transferred at 'close-of-play' yesterday evening.

It was picked up after just one ring. The tall, elegant but exceptionally gaunt man said nothing as he held the receiver to his ear.

The voice on the other end said just three words, "It is done."

The gaunt man said nothing, but he nodded gently as he replaced the receiver. The official notification would come through around 05:00, after the night nurse had made her next two-hourly check at 04:30. Then he would have to alert all the embassy staff. The Press Office would be busy and he himself would have to arrange the usual post-death necessities: the death certificate, the embalming, the coffin, the plane back to England (ironically somewhere she was allowed to return to only once since the abdication and exile in 1936, to attend her husband's funeral in 1972), the undertakers in the UK and even the burial next to her husband at Frogmore.

But for now he had time. He looked at his watch. She had said she wanted to know as soon as her instructions had been carried out. It was 02:30 in England and she would probably be asleep, but she would not take it kindly if he left it until the morning.

He picked the telephone back up, pressed the number for an outside line and then keyed the number for Clarence House in London...

PART ONE

Ω

FOUNDATIONS

Ω

Tuesday July 15 1997

Cyprus

Christina kept running. Running and running. Wildly at first, the pain in her head increasing with each stride until she thought she would pass out. The wide ethnic skirt entangled itself around her legs as she moved.

After half an hour her legs began to tire and she slowed to a walking pace, her breath coming uneasily. In a further fifteen minutes she had reached the village of Laxia. People seemed to be going about their business as normal, but there was an eerie quietness about the place. She accosted a villager and asked what had happened that morning, but the old woman just gave her a stony stare and hobbled on.

Christina came to the main Nicosia-Limassol road. The traffic seemed unusually thin, and what little of it there was was heading for Limassol, away from the capital. She had a nasty feeling that she knew exactly what was going on in Nicosia. Stelios had probably got embroiled in an attempt to overthrow Mouskos. She only hoped that he and Martinez had been successful, because such was the nature of their mission - to steal a diamond from the very person of Makarios - that they must either succeed or lose their lives.

Resting under a tree by the side of the road, she realised that her best bet lay back at the villa. Stelios would need her help - *if* he came back. *If it was ever Martinez' intention to have him come back.*

She accepted her thoughts with resignation. She had been near death too many times for the thought of it to horrify her any more, even the death of General George Grivas's son, her lover. But she must not run away. She must return to the villa to see what she could do.

As she arose a jeep thundered past her on the road, heading towards Nicosia. In the back she thought she saw one of the old EOKA members of the good old days, but the jeep had gone in a second in a cloud of dust, and she could not be certain. Not until days later did she realise that she had seen Nicos Sampson on his way to take up his short-lived Presidency.

She returned to the villa by the route she had come, half walking, half trotting.

Arriving back an hour later, the first thing she noticed was that the door of the place was ominously open, and there was not a sound from within...

Slowly, cautiously she looked inside. It took a moment for her eyes to adjust from the glaring sun outside to the dimness of the villa.

Then her hand shot to her mouth. *In the name of God, no!*

Her fears had been right.

Stelios Grivas lay on his back on the tiled floor, blood oozing from a gaping bullet wound in his chest. He was not moving and he was so, so pale. He was dead, he must be. She moved towards him.

Then something strange happened. Stelios opened his eyes. Smiling, he pulled himself up onto his elbows. "Hello, beautiful."

"Stelios?"

"He took the diamond, kid. That bastard double-crossed us, just like we thought he would." Carefully he got to his feet. Blood was flowing out of the hole in his chest, but he seemed not to notice.

"You are alive?" Christina could hardly believe it.

"Of course. It's not my time yet." He walked towards her. "I die later. Until then you must look after me. But we must contact our Controllers in Tel Aviv, let them know what happened. Come here, hold me - "

As he lifted his arms to embrace her, blood squirted straight outwards from his wound, spraying into Christina's face. She gasped as it went into her mouth and over her chin. She stepped back, tasting the heat of his blood, tasting the iron, tasting his life –

She sat up in bed choking, gasping for air. Her hair was matted with sweat, the bed sheet was saturated. Perspiration gleamed on her naked, fifty year old body.

"Stelios?" She looked around the dark bedroom. "S-Stelios…?"

But of course he was not there. It was the dream again.

No matter how many times she had it, it always seemed so real. She could smell Cyprus of 1974. She could feel the heat of Cyprus 1974. She could experience the pain of Cyprus 1974. She could hear the noise of Cyprus 1974 as President Makarios was overthrown and the island was divided, seemingly forever. She could taste her lover's blood…

She rolled over and grabbed her bottle of Evian from the bedside table. She went to put it to her lips but changed her mind and poured some of it over her head. Roughly she shook her still luxuriant long black hair, spraying water like a living fountain of Aphrodite.

This *was* still Cyprus. And this was one of the many properties she owned in the Hellenic Mediterranean. But this was *not* 1974.

It was 1997. Twenty-three years to the day since the Turkish invasion of Cyprus. Twenty-three years to the day since the island had been partitioned.

Twenty-three years to the day since Martinez – otherwise known as the Russian assassin Ilich Ramirov – had betrayed

Mossad Aliyah Beth...

Ω

Friday August 1 1997

Montmartre, Paris, France

The woman stood by the window of the apartment and watched the lights of Paris twinkle on beneath her. To her right the view from the *salle de jour* was obscured by the huge whitestone magnificence of Sacré Coeur on the crest of the *butte de Montmartre*. But just to the east, where the Basilica did not extend, she could see at an angle over the ridge with a view sweeping across to the towers of Notre Dame and beyond.

She sipped her Pernod and smiled silkily as the tabby cat wound itself in a figure of eight between her legs. This apartment had always belonged to a cat. Many years ago it had been Chivas, the long-haired black and white. But in the late eighties Chivas had missed her footing on one of her nightly sojourns across the rooftops of Montmartre, and she had plunged to her death onto Rue Lamarck below.

As if the cat world knew that a vacancy had arisen, a few months later Will, the female tabby, had appeared from nowhere and had stayed. She was called Will because when the woman had first noticed the cat perched perilously on the tiles outside, she had invited her in and asked her her name.

"Weeow," the cat had replied – and so Will it was.

The woman had been eighteen when her father had died, murdered not too far away from here. Two other men had also been killed at that time. One of them, a Chief Inspector of Police called Paul Richer, had been working with her father. Richer had owned this apartment. By a perversity that had never been explained, Richer had left this apartment to her father in his will. Richer had been killed just before her father, therefore the bequest was legal – even if her father never knew about his inheritance. The apartment had gone to her mother, who – after much family discussion on what to do with the place and whether to sell it – had agreed to let her daughter move in. That had been seventeen years ago, and she had lived there ever since.

Mother had died three years ago, and she had inherited in her own right.

She lived in the apartment alone – well, just her and Will. Just like any modern woman, men had come and gone in her life. Perhaps, she reflected ruefully, there had been too much coming and not enough going!

There had been one brief marriage, when she was young, impetuous and foolish. But she had soon got rid of him. None of her men (and she blanched inwardly when she thought of the quantity) had been the sort she would want to spend the rest of her life with. None of them matched up to The One – her father. Daddy. The man who had been her idol. The man who had been killed seventeen years ago. The man who was murdered, executed because he was who he was and he knew what he knew. The man who had never been avenged.

Until now.

She had waited all these years She knew she would know when the time was right. And it was now. She could feel it in her very being. Now, her father was calling out to her. It was time the world knew the truth. Time the world knew why her father had been murdered. Time the secret he had discovered and been killed for was revealed.

The quietness of the *salle de jour* was broken by a sharp, singular *crack*. The cat jumped but did not run away. It looked up and watched as the blood dripped down onto the fur on its back.

The woman looked at the broken glass in her hand. She felt no pain from the deep, bleeding laceration in her palm. Her only thought was that thank God she had finished her Pernod – it would have been a shame to waste good booze.

She raised her hand in the air and watched as the blood ran down her arm.

Yes, it had been long enough. It was time.

Time once again that the world heard the name Mesrine.

Ω

Monday August 4 1997

La Santé Prison, Paris, France

Eric Dejeune put his master key into the lock of the solid steel door of cell CS1 at 06:34 that morning. The cells in the solitary confinement block of the prison were locked and unlocked individually each day, there was no central locking unlike the cells in the main block.

And no central locking, thought Eric, unlike the doors on his new Honda Integra which he was taking delivery of that day. He smiled to himself as he thought of his new toy. He hoped this would be a usual, uneventful shift, he wanted to leave promptly at 14:00. No short notice overtime required today, thanks – he was picking up his new baby at 15:00.

He pushed the cell door open, hand on the holstered gun on his right hip. You always remembered your precautions, as trained – especially after, eighteen months previously, you had witnessed one of your colleagues literally have his head ripped off by one of these terrorist madmen whom the taxpayers of France kept in safety and relative luxury in what was colloquially known as The Mesrine Wing here in La Santé.

But this inmate was all right. World-famous he may be, responsible for the deaths of hundreds, but he had never been any trouble in the three years he had been here awaiting trial. A nice bloke, really.

"Bonjour Carlos," said Eric amiably as he entered the cell. "And what plans do you have this fine summer's day?"

The figure in the bed did not move. Normally he would be awake, ready to exchange quips.

Eric was instantly alert. "Carlos?" Instinctively his right hand clicked open the holster and pulled out the gun. "Ilych?" Slowly he moved towards the bed. He stopped a metre away and leant forward, prodding the figure with his gun. "Hey, Ramirez! Time to get up."

Nothing. Not a muscle. *Not a breath.*

Holding the gun rigidly in front of him, Dejeune carefully, gently, took hold of the blanket with his left hand. With a snap he whipped the blanket and underlying sheet off the bed Then he crouched in the defensive position, gun in both hands, finger on trigger, just as it said in the book.

He looked.

Then he sighed. The gun lowered as he straightened up.

Shit. *Shit, shit, shit.*

Bollocks.

Well, his car would have to wait now. Sod's bloody law. It was unbelievable. Today of all days!

The prisoner on the bed lay with his eyes open, jaw slack, tongue protruding, face frozen in agony. Ilych Ramirez Sanchez, also known as Carlos The Jackal, once the most feared man in the world, was as dead as a coffin nail.

Across The World

Time was, the death of the man who kept the world in fear in the 1970s and 80s would have warranted a News Flash on all major global television networks, maybe even an interruption of the scheduled programmes. But by 1997, Ilych Ramirez Sanchez – Carlos The Jackal – was a thing of the past, a hark-back to a bygone age when terrorism was in its infancy. His involvement in – and usually masterminding of – such things as the 1972 Olympics Massacre, the overthrow of Cyprus' President

Makarios in 1974 and the 1975 kidnapping of the OPEC oil ministers in Vienna – were now consigned to history, fiction and movies. Terrorism in the 1990s had moved on, atrocity after atrocity laying the foundations for the ultimate crescendo in 2001.

So the death of Ilych Ramirez Sanchez warranted no higher than the sixth item on Sky News and Fox News; on CNN it was item seven; ABC did not mention it at all. The bulletins were near-enough identical: the famous full-face picture (round chubby face, tinted glasses, hair black and wavy and pushed straight back), a Lufthansa jet being blown apart and a ten second shot of the gunmen in the Olympic Village in Munich in 1972.

Of the millions of people around the world who saw the news items, three had extreme reactions.

In Athens, Greece, Christina Cascianis burst into tears.

In Florida, USA, Ilich Ramirov was convulsed by paroxysms of laughter.

And in Tel Aviv, Israel, Chaim Cohen picked up the telephone.

Ω

Tuesday August 5 1997

14th Arrondisement, Paris, France

By their very nature, post mortems are brutal procedures. The effective skinning, carving and eviscerally-emptying of what was once a human being is for the strong of stomach only.

The autopsy on Ilych Ramirez Sanchez was particularly rough. No one, after all, would be claiming the body. It would just be put, piece by piece, into the furnace. Even as The Jaws were cracking open the ribcage, Dr Daniel Salinger could see that the heart had simply exploded. Not unknown. A natural death.

But nevertheless, Dr Salinger performed a full autopsy. The growing cult of Human Rights in the late 1990s, even here in France, meant that even someone like this *ordure* on the slab in front of him must have his final mortal examination meticulously documented.

Four hours later, just before the last piece of the body was thrown into the furnace, Dr Salinger picked up a pair of surgical scissors and did what he had been requested to do.

Through France

It was a filthy habit.

Dr Salinger had seen more deaths caused by these little

sticks, had cut open more tar-encoated lungs, than he could count. But still he took the last *mégot* from the packet of *Disques Bleues*, put it between his lips and lit up. He only just succeeded in holding in the cough. He was glad he had given up smoking years ago.

As the *TGV* train thundered through France from Paris to Lyons, he put the empty packet back in his pocket, thought better of it, pulled it back out again and threw it on the seat opposite.

A casual observer would have been curious as to why it was a *Disques Bleues* packet that went into the pocket but a *Gauloises* packet that ended up on the seat opposite. But there were no casual observers. There were just four other people in his part of the carriage: an old married couple (the man asleep, the woman reading a magazine); a young woman (headphones on, eyes closed, heading bobbing up and down to her music); and a business man (studying some papers).

As the train slowed towards its destination, La Part Dieu station in Lyons, Dr Salinger stood up and stretched. Wobbling with the movement of the train, he made his way forward, went through the internal doors and waited by the exit. Soon he would be checking in to the Carlton Hotel, and tonight he would have the finest meal on the menu at La Mère Brazier on Rue Royale. Tonight he would enjoy the most expensive wine available.

He was, after all, one million francs richer.

Back in the carriage, the old woman reached across and picked up the *Gauloises* packet from the seat. She placed it in her handbag and then went back to reading her magazine.

Under five hours later, the *Gauloises* packet was in Tel Aviv.

Ω

Wednesday August 6 1997

Troodos Mountains, Cyprus

"He iss gone, Stelios. At last, after all this time, he iss in hell where he belongs." Christina looked two metres to her right. "General, your son hass been avenged. *We* haf been avenged."

The sun beat down from the impossibly-blue sky. Even up here in the mountains – where it would start to snow in three months – it was hot. But the forty Celsius heat was well-tempered by the altitude. Down on the coast, the tourists would be sweltering and dropping.

The graves were in a sheltered clearing, in amongst the pine trees, well away from the main road. It was peaceful and naturally scented by the pines. Birds sang. Not many people now knew that there had once been a house on his spot. The house where the General had died on January 27 1974. Just two days after his death, the house had been razed by the Tactical Reserve Force of President Makarios. All but two people had died. At the time of the attack Christina and her lover, the General's son Stelios, had been higher up the mountain.

The summer Christina and Stelios had spent together had been... eventful. They had been on a quest, but they had been betrayed. Betrayed by the man whose death had been announced last week. By a man they knew then as Martinez. Only after Stelios' death had she discovered the true identity of the traitor: he was to become known to the world as Ilych Ramirez Sanchez, a Venezuelan idealist whom the Press would call Carlos The Jackal. In fact he was a Russian called Ilich Ramirov.

By that time she had also discovered that Stelios, a Cypriot Greek half-Jew, was also an agent of Israeli Intelligence. She had begged *Mossad Aliyah Beth* to let her help them find Ramirov. Initially they had refused. But over the years they had tested and utilised her, starting with little 'errands' until, many years later, she was trusted enough.

Ramirov had dropped out of sight at the end if the 1980s (it was even reported by some that he had died), cast adrift by his true masters upon the collapse of the USSR.

But the Jews never forget.

Information was gathered, analysed, retained, *remembered*. Israeli agents all over the world watched and waited. Like with the Nazis, the Israeli patience was long.

When Ramirov was kicked out of Syria in 1994, the Israeli machine was kicked back into life. Ramirov went to the Sudan where he thought he would be given sanctuary. But he was not. An Israeli tip-off to the French, a French 'word' with the Sudanese, and Ramirov was arrested in Khartoum on August 14 1994.

And watching in Sudan when he was arrested, and again in Paris when he arrived under heavy security, twenty years after the betrayal in Cyprus, was Israeli agent Christina Cascianis.

Officially General George Grivas, Head of EOKA and sworn enemy of Archbishop Makarios III, still lay where he was originally buried in the grounds of his house in Limassol. To this day the grave was tended by EOKA supporters, not all of them old.

Only a handful of people knew that the General had occupied the grave for little under a year. Upon the death of his son, he had been moved to the joint grave up here in the mountains, *his* mountains.

Christina knelt between the unmarked graves in the small

clearing. Leaning forward, she ran her hands simultaneously over both the rocks underneath which the dead father and son lay.

"It iss over," she said to them both, speaking in English for Stelios' sake, her accented Greek voice deep and mellow. "Now we can at last get on with our lifes." She turned to the rock on her left. "Stelios, iff only you had not left me. Think where we could haf been now. Think what Cyprus could haf been had you lived. The island would be united. We could haf had children…" Her eyes clouded.

Then she said briskly, "But, my dear, I yam too old for that now. And anyway you are nott here. And I never wanted children with any off the others."

She opened the small plastic bag she had brought with her and, as she did every month when she visited the graves, she upturned it and sprinkled flower petals over the two rocks. This month it was oleander, so she was careful not to touch the petals.

Then she stood up. It was time to go. "It iss over," she said again. "At last we can all rest in peace. I love you, my darling. I will see you next month." She turned and walked away.

Two metres underneath the rock on the left, the bones of Stelios Grivas began to scream.

PART TWO

Ω

ASSIGNMENTS

Ω

Thursday August 7 1997

Athens, Greece

Christina arrived back at her offices just off Platio Omónias at 11:00 the next day, travelling straight from Eleftherios Venezelos airport. Her assistant, the slim, dark haired Australian Teresa Cotton, and the three office staff were already at work and telephones were ringing. Business was good at *Cascianis Properties*.

Teresa was used to the Director's monthly trips to Cyprus – she owned six properties on the island (and another twenty around the Mediterranean) – so it was only right that she should make regular visits to inspect them. A hands-on approach. Good business practice. She did not know the real reason.

"Anything?" smiled Christina as she sat down behind her desk.

"The boys are handling the rentals," Teresa reported. "Corfu and Crete are now fully booked for the high season."

"Good, so is Cyprus."

"On the purchase side, there are another two properties about to come up in Campania - "

"Really? This is good. I would like more property in Southern Italy."

"I've e-mailed the details to you."

"Good girl, thank you."

"And Alex called. He will be in Athens next week. He asks if you could call him." Teresa raised her eyebrows as Christina smiled. She asked, "You two getting serious?"

"Serious? Alex? No, he is just a friend."

"A *friend…?*"

"Well… a girl has needs you know."

"Are the rumours about him true?"

"Rumours? What rumours?"

"About his wealth. About his account at Bank Christina and the regular deposits he makes?"

Teresa screamed as a handful of paperclips came hurtling towards her.

"You coarse child!" scolded Christina. "Pick those up and get back to your work! Wretched girl! I will haf you deported."

Three minutes later, smiling quietly to herself at the thought of the sex she would be having with Alex – at 35, fifteen years her junior and with appetites to match his age – she opened *Outlook Express*.

There were eight e-mails in her private account. Two of them were spam and five were from friends.

It was the eighth one that made the smile fall from her face. It was untitled. The sender address said *david5758@templenet.com*.

She hovered her mouse arrow over the message. Did she really want to see this?

Her right index finger moved and the message appeared on the screen. Just three words.

CONFESS YOUR SINS.

Ω

Saturday August 9 1997

Santuario del Carmine, Sorrento, Italy

"Bless me, Father, for I haf sinned. It hass been... many yearz since my last confession."

The inside of the wooden confessional in the south transept of the church of St Mary the Most Holy of the Carmine was musty, tainted with the breath – the sins – of the many penitents who over the years had sought absolution for their human frailties in this dark, claustrophobic upright tomb. The church was over 400 years old – and that was a lot of sins.

Only faint spears of light entered from the priest's side, through the grill that kept identities hidden, the sinner known only to God.

Christina could smell the priest's breath as he spoke. "And what have you to confess, my daughter?"

"Haf you got all day?" thought Christina. But out loud she gave the prearranged reply. "My search for justice hass made me many enemies."

"Vengeance is mine; I will repay, saith the Lord."

Christina waited on her knees in the darkness of the confessional. Outside she could hear the hardly subdued voices of the mostly English and German tourists wandering around the church, admiring the Neapolitan baroque-style architecture and the huge tapestries on the walls. Even though she was kneeling on a small hassock, her knees were beginning to hurt.

"It was not him," said the priest softly, speaking in English with the sibilant hiss of his real race.

"What wass not him?" asked Christina, puzzled.

"The death, in Paris - "

Christina stiffened.

" – The body. It was not him."

After a moment she said, "How do you know?"

"We have suspected the trick for some time," explained the priest. "But until now we have not been able to prove it. We obtained a hair sample from the body before it was… disposed of. The DNA does not match the blood he left behind in Amsterdam."

"But hiss fingerprints - "

"Can be forged. False prints can be worn or grafted. Or base records can even be changed. You know what the west's idiotic police and security forces are like. But the Amsterdam DNA we have kept to ourselves all these years. And it does not match up. The man held in prison in France was not him. It never was him."

Christina was perplexed. "But I wass there when he was picked up in Khartoum."

"Yes."

"And I was there to see him off the plane in Paris."

"But you were not on the plane."

"What?"

"We think that was where the switch was made."

"But how could that possibly have been done?"

"Collusion."

"But he wass cuffed and manacled, surrounded by French agents – " Christina stopped as realisation hit home. The face on the other side of the grill said nothing. "So," she said slowly, " the French let him go…?"

"Yes."

"But why?"

"Who knows? This is the French we're talking about."

"My God." Softly.

"It has been done many times before. Churchill, Stalin, Roosevelt, Makarios – even today, Saddam Hussein. They were all known to use doubles. An effective ploy. The public sees what it wants to see, it believes what it wants to believe. If it is told that Roosevelt met with Churchill in the Hamptons, if it is shown a photograph that purports to be Roosevelt and Churchill meeting in the Hamptons, then Roosevelt and Churchill have met in the Hamptons. Carlos is arrested and taken on a plane, therefore it must be Carlos that is taken off that plane."

"I know how it works." There was a hard edge to Christina's voice. "But why are you telling me this? I haf not had contact with Tel Aviv for two yearz. Ramirov iss not likely to come after me."

"No, he is not one for vengeance. He would not consider you worthy. I am telling you this because you were instrumental in his capture. Or rather in his non-capture. You failed. And we, my dear, *are* ones for vengeance. As of this moment, Agent Cascianis, you are back on active duty."

"But I am fifty yearz old!"

The priest ignored her protest. "As before, our worldwide network will be at your disposal. You were recruited twenty years ago with one ultimate goal. You have not achieved that goal. You have not given us a return on the investment we made in you. As Jews, we do not like that.

"Achieve your goal, Cascianis. Find him. And this time end it once and for all."

Circolo dei Forestieri, Sorrento, Italy

Christina sat alone at a table on the wide terrace of the *Circolo dei Forestieri*, looking out over Sorrento's Marina Piccolo below. Her eyes travelled across the blue water of the Mediterranean to the huge, imposing bulk of Mount Vesuvius on the other side of the Bay of Naples.

It was the height of the holiday season, and very soon the Foreigners' Club – the restaurant, café, bar, nightclub, and tourist information centre that had been one of the main hubs of Sorrento's holiday industry for over 40 years – would be filling with lunchtime diners.

But at 10:30 she had the place almost to herself. There were a few early clients for cappuccino (maybe with a slice of delicious lemon cake), and over on the other side of the terrace a group of about a dozen newly-arrived vacationers sat in rapt awe of a holiday company rep giving her introductory spiel (and hoping to sell some lucrative local tours) for probably the fiftieth time that season.

The sun was high in the sky behind her – soon for the three hours of midday it would be impossible to sit out in. Even now the heat was increasing minute by minute, and although she wore just a sleeveless low-cut blue and white cotton dress, she had made a point of sitting at a table with a sun parasol.

She was waiting for the next contact. The 'priest' had told her where to go on leaving the church, and he had said she would be contacted almost immediately.

Her espresso was delivered. The waiter, wearing the name 'Tony', put her *conto* underneath the small wooden block on the table. A small, wrapped piece of dark chocolate sat against the cup on the saucer, and Christina took it out of the foil packaging and popped it in her mouth.

"Christina?"

She looked up. The woman was around fifty, shoulder-length red wavy hair falling from under a wide straw hat, large sunglasses covering her freckled face. She wore a loose red and green open flowered blouse with the top of a dark green one piece swimsuit showing underneath. A loose elastic-waisted red skirt fell to her calves, stopping above cream espadrilles. A straw bag was over her shoulder.

Christina took it all in, especially the friendly face, and then said "My search for justice hass made me many enemies."

The woman smiled. "Vengeance is mine; I will repay, saith the Lord." She sat down. "Hi, I'm Melanie." Her accent was straight English.

Christina nodded. "Excuse me iff I seem confused. This iss all a bit of a shock."

"I understand. It must be. It was for me, too."

Christina looked surprised. "You know him? Martinez? Sorry, I still use that name. *Ramirov?*"

"Oh yes, I know him." Melanie thought back over the years and of what she had done for Israel. "I thought you'd captured him. Then, like you, I thought he was dead."

"But how – " Christina stopped as the waiter came up behind them. She asked, "Melanie, can I get you something?"

"Er – cappuccino, please."

The waiter nodded, wrote on his small pad, and departed.

"But how the hell am I supposed to - " Christina made bunny ears with the index and middle fingers of both hands " 'find him'? He could be anywhere in the world. It iss not like he just escaped from jail five days ago, he hass been out there all this time, all these yearz. It iss impossible."

"Do you not want to be the one who finally finishes him?"

"Until an hour ago I thought I was."

"And now?"

"Now?" Christina sighed. "That bastard ruined my life. I should have shot him when I could, instead of handing him over to the French." She looked across the bay at the sleeping giant of the volcano. "He should be dead. And yess, I would like it to be me that does it." She turned back. "But we have to be realistic here. I am fifty yearz old. I am not the young girl I wass."

"Neither am I," Melanie smiled.

"I would not know where to start."

The cappuccino was delivered and a second *conto* was slipped beneath the wooden block.

"Things are different nowadays," explained Melanie as she undid the packet of sugar and emptied it onto the froth. "Technology is advancing at an astonishing rate. Previously we had to use people on the ground. Tails, phone taps, you name it. Remember we found Ramirov for your Stelios before?"

"You were involved in that?"

"I had… some input, yes. Well all that with people on the ground is old hat. Nowadays you can trace anyone – and I mean *anyone*, even if they do not want to be traced. It is still not easy, but it is much more sophisticated."

"What do we need?"

"A computer."

"A computer?"

"And the technology which only we have. Even the mighty US is way behind us." Melanie reached out and took Christina's hand. "You want to find Ilich Ramirov?"

"Oh, *yes*."

"And this time finish it once and for all?"

Christina nodded, biting her lower lip.

"Then we shall do it," said Melanie with firm conviction. "We might be older but we are still trained operatives. And now we have the resource."

"But why us?"

"Tel Aviv trusts us. And they are Jews. They believe in an eye for an eye. They believe in the right of revenge. The right for you to avenge our agent Digenis – your Stelios Grivas."

Christina's eyes filled. Then she waved over the waiter.

"*Signora?*" asked Tony.

"You don't," asked Christina, "happen to haf a cigar, do you?"

"*Prego, signora.* What kind?"

"Something long, thick and utterly disgusting should suit me just fine," she said.

Ω

Sunday August 10 1997

Capodichino Airport, Naples, Italy

At 10:00 that morning Melanie and Christina met up as planned in the food court upstairs in the departure area of the airport.

The two women had gone their separate ways after their meeting at the Foreigners' Club yesterday: Melanie back to her hotel (the *President,* high up on the cliffs) via a brief spot of pre-arranged confession in the *Santuario del Carmine,* and Christina back to the *immobiliare* on the Corsa Italia to finalise a property purchase (she still had a business to run).

Christina spent the night at the *La Solara* hotel out on Via Capo (enjoying the legendary hospitality of owner Ugo di Maio and his staff), and in the morning her pre-ordered taxi collected her at 08:30 for the ninety minute journey to Napoli.

At 11:00 the women boarded the Alitalia plane for the 30 minute flight to Rome.

Fiumicino, Rome, Italy

Being an internal flight, there were no formalities at Leonardo da Vinci Airport, and the two women were in the unmarked, untraceable embassy Fiat Cinquento twenty minutes after landing.

"Can we talk detail now?" asked Christina as they moved out

into the traffic on the A12.

"Sure," said Melanie. "No one to overhear us now. And the car is clean."

"So, we use a computer?"

"Yep."

"And this computer can track down anybody in the world?"

"Give or take. With the right knowledge. *Hey! Up your Mama!*" She gave the finger to a grinning, unhelmeted youth on a Vespa.

"And what knowledge would that be?"

"You'll see."

"This must be one hell of a computer. Must be huge. Where is it? Underneath the Coliseum? Beneath St Peter's Square?"

"No, it's in my apartment. It's my laptop."

Via Catalana, Rome, Italy

Melanie's apartment was in an old block dating back to before Il Duce. While Christina showered, Melanie made up a spare camp bed in the *soggiorno*. When Christina came out of the bathroom, wearing just a towel, a pair of fresh cotton day jammies (white T shirt and blue gingham shorts) were awaiting her. Then it was Melanie's turn to shower and change, into red day jammies.

While coffee brewed in the small, basic kitchen, Melanie removed her *Compaq* from a shelf and took it over to her coffee table.

"Don't know why they call these things laptops – that's the one place you can't put them. More than five minutes and they burn your bloody legs off!" She plugged the machine into the mains for constant power, and connected another wire into the back.

Christina's eyes traced the second wire to another socket in the wall. To the casual eye this looked just like a telephone internet connection – except Melanie's phone was plugged in on the other side of the room. This connection was stand alone and dedicated. Melanie saw her looking. "Ever heard of Broadband?" she asked.

Christina shook her head.

"Not many people have. But you will." Melanie left the computer to warm up and went back to the kitchen.

Christina looked at the thirty-eight centimetre screen coming slowly to life. She wondered how the hell this little machine was going to help them locate one person in the world. She said as much to Melanie when she returned with two cups of coffee and an opened packet of Grisbi crème biscuits.

"Barking Dog," the Englishwoman replied.

"Excuse me?"

"We have had it for a while now." A Grisbi crumb stuck to Melanie's chin, but she did not seem to notice. "It's more than a program. I suppose you could call it a *development*. Nobody else has it to the extent that we do. It gives us the technological edge – and therefore the information edge – over all our enemies."

"I can't imagine Saddam and Assad having huge IT resources." Christina reached over and brushed the crumb from her colleague's face.

"Thanks," said the Englishwoman. "You would be surprised. Even Arafat in his poor little bombed-out compound has technological resources that would amaze you. But I said *all* our enemies."

"All?"

"This is far in advance of anything even the Americans, Russians or Chinese have."

Christina raised her eyebrows, trying to conceal her doubt. "So how does it work?"

"Why have a dog and bark yourself?" smiled Melanie.

"Sorry?"

"Barking Dog. Why should we gather and store information when others will do it for us?" Melanie saw the confusion on the Greek woman's face and she rubbed her arm. "We have developed an instant universal hacker. Our little baby gives us access to *any* computer, any network, any server, any hardware, any software, *anywhere*. Even in space. We don't need user IDs, passwords, code words or whatever. Barking Dog has already done that for us and has by-passed all security, firewalls, defences, you name it. And afterwards the host has no idea we have even been there. Barking Dog leaves no trace. Like a thief in the night." She laughed. "I sound like a saleswoman, don't I?"

"But if this effer got into the wrong hands...?"

"It would not work. It would be useless. 'Hands' is right." Melanie held up the first two fingers of her right hand. "Ever heard of biometric access?"

"Er, no."

Melanie put her two fingers on what looked like a second mousepad on the computer. Slowly she ran them across the pad twice.

The screen flickered and began to metamorphose.

"Welcome to Barking Dog," said Melanie. "You now have access to every computer in the world." She turned to the Greek woman. "So, where shall we start looking? More coffee, hun? This will take some time."

Ω

Monday August 11 1997

Rue Le Regrattier, Île St Louis, Paris, France

"You are not Susanne."

The old man with the hideously scarred scalp and face manoeuvred his wheelchair back from the front door of the apartment so that the nurse could enter.

"*Susanne est en vacances*," explained the woman as she came in. "She told you last week she was going away, don't you remember?" She spoke with the slightly condescending attitude of nurse to patient, but with just a hint of the coquette.

"Did she? I am sure you are right."

The old man wheeled himself into the salon and then turned to face the nurse. Even in his eighties, he could appreciate a pretty woman. And this one was indeed *belle*. She wore no make-up (which he found attractive), and the figure underneath the plain white button-through nurse's dress looked perfect – at least to an old man like him. He detested the skinny-Minnie look of the young women nowadays. Real women should have curves – and this one had them. She was not big, but the curves were in all the right places. He glanced down at her legs; they were clad in black hose. He might have imagined it, but did he have a long forgotten feeling in a long forgotten part of his anatomy?

"And you are?" he asked.

"My name is Florence," she smiled as she set down her case. In front of her she saw a man dressed casually but elegantly in fawn *pantalon* with a matching jacket over a white shirt, a front of respectability and culture, maintained despite the disability. A lightly patterned dark brown cravat around his neck harked back to another time – his time, which was long ago now.

His scarred and crimson head looked raw even after all these years, and there were about three strands of hair brushed over the top of it. The scarring continued over his forehead and down the right side of his face.

"*Et ma belle Florence*, you have come to give me my bed bath, no?" The watery old eyes twinkled.

"I don't think that is in the contract," she scolded. "How are we this week?"

"*We?* Well, I don't know about you but I still live. I suppose that makes *ça va*."

"Do you want me to take you for your walk?"

"Time was, if a beautiful young lady like yourself was alone with me in my apartment, going for a walk would be the last thing on our minds."

"Time is, not was, m'sieur. Come, where do you keep your blanket? An hour in the fresh air will do you good."

Le Jardin des Tuileries, Paris, France

Although it was a fine Parisian Monday and the sun shone, he was still dressed in jacket, shirt and cravat and now had the blanket over his legs, suffering from the permanent chill of age. A wide-brimmed hat covered his face from the casual passer-by.

She had wheeled him for twenty minutes, much to his annoyance. When she was behind him he could not admire her shapely body. She was just a disembodied voice, talking in the condescending '*nous*' format. "Are we too warm in that jacket? How are we feeling now we're out?"

Finally she parked the wheelchair alongside a seat in the Tuileries Gardens, facing the eastern pond. She sat down next to him. She smiled. "There now. Let us spend a little time here and then we will go back."

"Susanne usually reads to me," he said. "My eyes, they are not very good with words nowadays."

"Well, Susanne will be back next week. I have nothing to read to you. How about if we just talk?"

He sighed, "Yes, let us talk then *ma belle*." His hand reached out and patted her knee. She made no move to remove it. "Tell me about yourself," he said.

"Me? Oh, I'm not that interesting. I will tell you about myself later. Maybe when we get back to your apartment you can get to know me better."

His heartbeat quickened. Had he heard her correctly?

"Tell me about *you*," she said. "Do you mind talking about it?"

"About what?"

She motioned with her hand to her own face. "Your accident."

"Accident! Pah!" The old man raised his croaky voice. "This was deliberate. Eighteen years ago. They tried to kill us all. But I survived. They thought they'd burned us all to death, but I was saved. Trapped under the beam." He sniffed ruefully. "The same beam that broke my back also saved my life!"

He stopped talking as a group of Japanese tourists passed by. His hand was still on her knee, and now she covered it with her cardigan. Was it his imagination or did she jog his hand higher?

"We only have the medical background at the agency," she explained. "No history of the cause of the trauma. But Susanne mentioned you were a policeman?"

"I was a Commissaire. I had my own section, the BCP – *Bureau de la Co-opération Politique*. I set it up." His grip on her thigh relaxed as he reminisced. "It is still going strong today…"

"And this happened to you because of case you were working on?"

The old man said nothing. His chin shook gently and drool

rolled slowly from the corner of his burnt mouth. The nurse reached across and wiped it with a tissue. Liquid filled his already watery eyes.

Then he said resolutely, "*Oui et non*. I do not wish to discuss it further."

She was quiet, looking at the children sailing their boats on the pond. She turned to him. "Do you want to go home?"

"*S'il te plait.*"

She re-tucked in the blanket. Instead of taking the wheelchair brake off with her foot, she leant forward to do it manually. As she bent down her face was only centimetres from his. "Now *you* can get to know *me*," she said.

Rue Le Regrattier, Île St Louis, Paris, France

When they re-entered the apartment a red light was flashing on the old man's telephone, but they both ignored it. She helped him remove his hat and jacket and then offered to make them coffee, but the old man refused. "Let us have a cognac, there is a bottle over there."

She went over to the wooden drinks cabinet and retrieved a bottle of *Otard*. He admired her rump as she leant forward. "So tell me about yourself," he said to her bottom. "You said I could get to know you better."

She turned back, smiling. "*D'accord*. It is only fair. But first you tell me just one last thing, Colonel."

The smile dropped from his face. Nobody had addressed him like that in eighteen years.

"How did you know - ?"

"I know a lot of things, Colonel." She was standing in front of him, legs apart. She had undone the bottom two buttons on her dress. The bottle of *Otard* was in her hand. "You are Commissaire Charles Fleury-Goujon. You were also Colonel and Commander-in-Chief of the OAS. My father died for you."

"Y- your father?" Fear mingled with lust as he stared at her left thigh.

"They were all working for you. Trying to find the secret. And they all died."

Instantly he was transported back eighteen years. Slowly, he said "It – it was not my fault. It was Richer. And that meddling fool Gerard. We were so close to getting the secret."

"What is the secret, Colonel?"

"What?"

"The secret. What is it?" She straddled his useless legs and sat down on his knees, the dress riding up her thighs. The brakes were on and the wheelchair remained stable.

He looked between her legs. Although she wore the black pantyhose, he could see she wore no other underwear.

"The secret?" He was drooling again. "How should I know? Richer would not tell me. He said it was for my own good that I did not know."

"But you were attacked."

"Afterwards. The British were mopping up, they obliterated the OAS High Command - just in case we knew."

"Just in case?" She took the cork out of the bottle. "That must be some secret. For the British to kill you all *just in case* you might know."

His right hand shook as he gently touched her inner thigh. It had been such a long time since he had touched a woman. He said softly, "We never knew – " Then he stopped. He took his eyes from her sex, squashed inside her tights, and looked at her face.

"Your father...?" He said thoughtfully. Then his head jumped backwards. "Oh my God. You look like him. *Him?* I didn't think - "

"What you think does not matter, Colonel. It is what you *know* that matters. What is the secret everyone must die for?"

"I don't know."

"What can be so terrible?"

"*Je ne sais pas.* If I did, do you think I would be a lonely old man living here?"

"The Brits would not have killed you all otherwise."

"They did not kill *me.*"

"As good as. They certainly kept you quiet. You know the secret and you will not tell me." She noticed his eyes go back down to between her legs. "You want this, don't you?" She moved her hips back and forth against his useless legs. "Would you like to try?"

"A – a man of my age can only reminisce. And dream."

"What is the secret? Tell me and you can touch me. Would you like to kiss me there? To taste me? You know you want to. I will let you. Just tell me. What is the secret?"

There was deep regret in the watery eyes. "Not even for your delights, *ma belle.*"

Abruptly she stopped moving. "Do not '*ma belle*' me, Colonel."

"What do you want me to call you?" he sneered. "*Ma poule?*"

"Call me Mesrine."

He took a deep breath. "Mesrine," he said the name to himself.

"So, you won't tell me," she said pleasantly as she stood up, and Charles Fleury-Goujon looked at a woman's sex for the very last time.

"No." Gruffly, defiantly.

"Well, it does not matter. You have had eighteen years more life than my father, so we can at least rectify that."

"What do you mean, you little whore - " He lashed out with his arm, but she had stepped out of reach and had moved behind him.

Then his raw scalp began to rage as he felt her pour the cognac over his head.

"What - what are you doing?" He shouted, hands grasping for the wheelchair brake lever.

From her bag she produced a lighter and a bandage.

Fleury shook his head as the alcohol stung his eyes. He released the brakes and tried to turn towards her.

Calmly she lit the bandage.

"For my father," she said, and dropped the bandage onto his head.

She did not stop to see Charles Fleury-Goujon engulfed by flames for the second time in his life. As his screaming got louder and louder and she began to smell meat cooking, she calmly picked up her bag and left the apartment, closing the front door after her.

The Colonel was just a screaming fireball in the centre of the room. He pushed himself up off the wheelchair, but his useless legs crumbled beneath him.

The screaming stopped as the fireball settled on the floor, a living cremation.

And then the fireball began to move. Slowly, it rolled across the room. Could a whimpering be heard? It stopped by the table near the door. Bit by bit the fireball raised itself up. A human hand stretched upwards and outwards from it. It grabbed the telephone and brought it crashing down onto the floor.

Trembling, blistering, the fingers keyed a seven digit number. From the fireball came an inhuman sound. "Me- Me- Mer. Me- Me- Me-. Mesrine! Mesrine! Mesrine - "

Then the sound stopped.

The hand poking from the fireball twitched once violently and was still, succumbing to the flames.

The final twitch of the hand knocked against the telephone, which began to play the message on the ansaphone. A message which fell on dead ears.

"Allo? Allo, Monsieur Fleury-Goujon? This is the Saint Marie Nursing Agency. I am sorry but Susanne will not be with you today. She has not called into the office. I don't know what can be wrong with her. Regretfully we have no other nurses

available at such short notice, but if you would care to call us we can arrange for somebody to visit you tomorrow. *Merci bien, monsieur, bonjour."*

Rue des Saussaies, Paris, France

Chief Inspector Pierre Jamo was alone in the Inspectors' Office of the BCP suite at 11 Rue des Saussaies when the telephone rang. He was halfway through reading a report about a Brazilian diplomat with transsexual proclivities, so he reached for the receiver absentmindedly.

"Jamo."

At first it just sounded like interference on the line, a crackling sound. Then he heard, "Me- Me- Mer. Me- Me- Me-. Mesrine! Mesrine! Mesrine - " It stopped suddenly and was followed by a gurgling sound. It was a human voice, definitely. But the gurgling following the words was inhuman. Then that too stopped abruptly. Then the call was disconnected.

The black haired, fortyish policeman frowned at the phone in his hand. What the hell was that?

Since the débâcle many years ago which had led to internal treachery and the consequent deaths of both the Chief Inspectors of the BCP, all incoming calls were recorded. Although nowadays there was only one Chief Inspector in the unit (*lui-même*), because of the diplomatically sensitive nature of the BCP's work, the tradition of recording incoming calls had been maintained. It was a fact known only to the Chief Inspector and his Commissaire – therefore giving the additional bonus of it being a management check on the staff.

What the staff did know was that all calls inwards on the unit's direct lines were automatically caller identified. Jamo picked his telephone back up and keyed the General Office.

The veteran Sergeant Maurice Goise answered.

"Maurice," said Jamo. "The last call to my line, a minute ago.

Do we have a number?"

"I will look for you, Chief Inspector..." Goise was back within thirty seconds. "I have it here."

"*Alors*, try it for me will you? And get me a name and address."

"*D'accord*, Chief Inspector."

Jamo pressed the cradle on his telephone and then let it pop up again. He keyed the four digit security number known only to him and the Commissaire.

An automated, computerised female voice, deep and authoritative, said "Please enter your personal identification number."

Jamo pressed six figures.

"Please enter the extension number required."

He keyed his own four digit number.

"Please enter the number of hours required, maximum forty-eight."

He keyed 1.

There was the merest pause, and then the voice said in a more disjointed fashion. "There have been – *three* - calls on this number in the last – *one* - hours. Press five to hear the first call. Press three to listen to the next call."

Jamo pressed 5 and heard the beginning of a call he had received from the Vietnamese Embassy fifty minutes ago. He pressed 3. The next call was from a picture framers up on Boulevard Haussmann (he had left a Robert Heindel print to be reframed a couple of days ago). He pressed 3 again.

The voice said, "Call received at - *fifteen forty-three* - hours, - *Monday August Eleven.*" A pause. Then came the crackling sound. Then, "Me- Me- Mer. Me- Me- Me-. Mesrine! Mesrine! Mesrine - " Then the gurgling.

Jamo pressed the back arrow on the handset and listened to the message again. Then again. And again.

The voice was high. Was it male or female? It sounded old or distressed, or maybe both. Probably male then. "Me- Me– Mer."

It could have been the personal pronoun, but it was more likely to be the preliminary attempts to utter the word that followed. "Mesrine! Mesrine! Mesrine – "

There was no mistaking it. *Mesrine*. The surname of the most notorious criminal France had ever produced. *Jacques Mesrine*. The man who, eighteen years previously, had been working on an assignment for Chief Inspector Paul Richer of the BCP, even as the combined mights of all the Police forces of France were hunting him. It was a mission that had ended up with both Paul Richer and his colleague Claude Gerard dead, and Mesrine executed publicly by Bouvier and his crew.

Despite internal enquiries, it had never been discovered what exactly Mesrine was doing for the BCP. There were rumours it was something to do with the British, but there was no conclusive evidence. All the protagonists had died in November 1979. The BCP Commissaire at the time, Charles Fleury-Goujon, knew only that Richer was engaged in recovering some jewellery stolen from the American woman, the so-called Duchess of Windsor. Richer had been working to his own agenda. And then, ironically, three days after the deaths of Richer and Mesrine and two days after the death of Claude Gerard, Fleury-Goujon had been paralysed and severely burnt in a fire at a Masonic lodge meeting up in Belleville.

They must have been crazy times…

The ringing of the telephone snapped Jamo out of his reveries.

"*Oui?*"

"Goise, sir. I tried the number but I cannot get a connection. It might have gone out of service or something. But I have the name and address for you. The call came from a telephone situated at 15 Rue Le Regrattier in the 4th, on the Île St Louis. The subscriber – wait for it – is our old friend and Commissaire, Charles Fleury-Goujon."

Ω

Jamo was quiet.

"Sir?" said Sergeant Goise. "Chief Inspector?"

"Mm? Yes, thank you, yes."

"Quite something after all these years, old Charlie Boy ringing. I wonder what he wanted? Did he leave a message on your Voicemail?"

"Yes, er, oh it was nothing important. Silly bugger didn't leave his name, that's why I asked you to check. I think the old boy was just getting nostalgic."

"I remember him well," reminisced Goise. "Shame, what happened to him. He was the first and the best of our bosses. Not like that career minded bitch we have now."

Jamo thought of the recently-appointed Commissaire Gillian Colet, 'The only woman who can travel further on her back than standing up' as she was known around Saussaies. But he decided to say nothing. He humphed and put the phone down.

From his top drawer he withdrew his new-fangled mobile telephone. He extended the aerial, managed to get into his ten number phone memory at the third attempt, located the person he wanted and pressed the green 'Call' key.

After ten seconds the person at the other end answered. As always on these things, it was a bad reception.

"Inspector Ibrahim," Jamo raised his voice. "I want you to get down to the Île St Louis. Rue Le Regrattier. Number fifteen. I will meet you there." Jamo looked out of the office window at the top of the Palais d'Elysée two blocks beyond. Still on the telephone he said, more lowly "I think history may be calling us."

Rue Le Regrattier, Île St Louis, Paris, France

The street was quiet. Although the summer sun gave a warm evening ambience, its rays touched only the upper parts of the old buildings on the west side of the rue at this time of day and did not reflect downwards to street level.

Pierre Jamo sat in his dirty white Fiat Uno and surveyed number 15. There were no ambulances about, no bystanders, no gawpers, no commotion to indicate anything had happened here today. It was just a quiet street on the elegant Île St Louis.

He climbed out of his car and smoothed his short, cropped black hair. His grey suit jacket (which had seen better days even when better days had seen better days) hung open above his white, open necked shirt. His shoulder-holster and gun could be seen clearly.

He looked up as he heard a noise from down the road. A Ducati M900 motorbike turned in from the Quai de Bourbon and roared the wrong way down this one-way street. It stopped with a squeal of brakes, double-parking next to his Fiat.

Jamo raised his eyebrows as the person in biking leathers, boots and red crash helmet climbed off the bike.

"Nice of you to turn up," said Jamo with Gallic dryness.

The rider removed the helmet and ruffled the short brown hair beneath.

"Hello Chief. What's the panic? Where's the fire?" quipped Inspector Claudette Ibrahim.

The front door to the building was unlocked and the concierge was out. There was a distinct smell of someone's dinner permeating the entrance hall.

There were two apartments on the *rez de chaussée*, and the one they wanted was obvious by the added ramp leading up to the front door.

"I had a phone call an hour ago," Jamo explained. "Traced it here."

"You had a phone call and you needed to trace it?" queried Claudette, rubbing her short hair again to let it breathe after its session under the helmet.

"A strange phone call. Didn't leave his name. You know who lives here?"

"*Mais non,* of course not."

Jamo knocked on the door. "Have you heard of one of our old Commissaires, Fleury-Goujon?"

Claudette frowned. "Name rings a bell."

"You were probably still at school - "

She smiled.

" – or at least at the Academy." Jamo knocked again. "The first Commissaire of the BCP. Commissaire!" he called. "*Sûreté!* Bay-Say-Pay!"

"*Ah mais oui!*" Claudette unbuttoned her leather jacket. Her shoulder holster was visible above her black T shirt. "Wasn't he the one who was done in that fire?"

"That's him." This time Jamo used his fist on the door instead of his knuckles. "Commissaire!" He turned to Claudette. "Try the other apartment, will you?"

Claudette went over and knocked smartly on the identical door on the other side of the hallway. She looked back at Jamo. "Also he was in charge when those Chief Inspectors were killed."

"The Mesrine affair," nodded Jamo.

"Oui. La Conclusion." She knocked again. Nothing. "It seems everyone's out on a Monday evening."

"Well, someone around here is cooking - " Jamo stopped. He turned back to the door. *Oh my God.* "We need to get in." He pushed against the door. "*Now!*" He stepped back two paces and rammed his shoulder against the wood.

"Get out of the way." Claudette pushed his chest with her hand. "Mind." Her booted right foot slammed into the door, and it flew open with a splinter of wood.

The smell of cooking tumbled out to meet them.

"Commissaire!" called Jamo as they both entered with their Glock 17 handguns drawn. They stood either side of the salon door to the left. Jamo reached out, looked at his partner, turned the handle and pushed the door open.

Claudette crouched down, gun in both hands pointing in

front of her, peering into the room The smell was now overwhelming. Then she said "Oh fuck," and stood up. Jamo looked over her shoulder.

On the burnt carpet near the door lay what could have been a discarded, barbecued pig, well done and crackling. The mouth was open as if it had been spit-roasted, but there was no apple in it. The flesh was so dark, it could have been honey-basted. But at the lower end of the object was the evidence that this was not an indoor feast.

Lying where the flames had not reached were the bottom of two human legs, encased in *pantalon*, *chaussettes* and brown formal men's shoes.

"In the name of Mary," said Pierre Jamo. He pulled a packet of *Gauloises* from his pocket and then, noting Claudette's look of disapproval, put them away again. Perhaps this was not the right place and time to light up.

"Is this him?" she asked.

"How the fuck should I know?" he replied. "He doesn't quite match his 'Class of 79' picture in the year book any more."

"What's going on, Chief?"

Jamo noticed the telephone on the floor near the body.

"I think," he said. "We may have a problem."

Montparnasse, Paris, France

"So you are leaving it all to the *Police Judiciaire*," said Inspector Claudette Ibrahim in a slightly mocking tone.

"What else can I do?" reasoned Chief Inspector Pierre Jamo. "It is a murder. It is their territory. We are the BCP. The *Bureau de la Co-opération Politique*. Unless the murder has a diplomatic involvement, it is not ours to investigate."

"But he was our ex-Chief, isn't that enough?"

"He hasn't been our Chief for eighteen years. He was just a

retired old man, a civilian."

She sighed. "I know you are right. The poor bastard. Burnt to death twice! What about this Mesrine thing?"

"I don't know. What I do know is that Mesrine has been lying in his grave next to his father up in Clichy for eighteen years too. If he was going to come back and seek revenge, he would have done it long before now!"

"Perhaps it was just a dying thing."

"What was?"

"The Chief. You know, how some people when they're dying see a tunnel with a bright light at the end of it and people waiting for them. Perhaps the Chief saw Mesrine."

"Hardly a loved one!"

"Maybe it's different for us *flics*. Maybe we see all the people we've put away!" She chuckled. Then she said reflectively, "Or all the people we've killed."

"Well that's something you and I won't have to worry about for a long time. You got anything pressing in the morning?"

"Nothing pressing."

"*Bon*. Then you don't have to go home just yet."

"Not just yet."

She turned towards him on his bed and they began to kiss.

Ω

Tuesday August 12 1997

Clarence House, London, England

The matriarch of the British Royal Family was now ninety-seven years old. But despite her vast age, her mental faculties were all intact – there was not, and would never be, any hint of senility. Physically she was beginning to suffer the debilitation of old age (much more than the public realised), but her muscular and skeletal condition was still that of a person twenty years younger.

God, fate and history would decree that she had almost another five years to live, that she would live for over a full calendar century and see in the new millennium.

But she did not know that.

That day she thought she was dying.

Respiratory problems, palpitations and hypertension had given her a series of 'funny turns'. The last one at lunchtime that day was so bad that she had passed out. She had awoken in her bedroom with her consultant, a nurse, her junior secretary and Billy the butler standing around her bed.

As with all unconsciousness, the hearing was the last to go and the first to come back. So her return to the land of the living was not immediately accompanied by any physical movement or other outward signs, and the people around her bed did not know she had returned. Not that it would have mattered if they had, they were having a normal conversation about the patient's condition.

The actual conversation went as follows:

"What is Her Majesty's condition?" The secretary.

"Satisfactory. There is nothing to concern us," her consultant. "She is not dying yet! Such things must be expected. She is strong and will outlive us all! And don't be afraid to tell her I said so when she wakes up. I have given her a mild sedative."

What Her Majesty heard in her wakening state was:

"Her Majesty's condition?"

"There is concern. She is dying. Be strong. Don't tell her."

And that was why three hours later, when she was alone and fully conscious, she summoned Sir Kenneth Dean to her bedchamber.

Sir Kenneth Dean was a tall, elegant but exceptionally gaunt man, a product of pre-war Eton. The position of 'Senior Secretary' and the accompanying knighthood were created for him eleven years previously as a reward for services rendered to Her Majesty Queen Elizabeth the Queen Mother.

He had duties, of course, mostly the supervision of security surrounding HM. But he would have been the first to admit that the position was virtually a sinecure.

Now he attended Her Majesty, as requested. At four o'clock, "Just after tea."

She was sitting in her high-backed armchair in her bedroom, looking out over the inner garden.

"Marm? You asked for me." Sir Kenneth maintained the deference and respect due to the old lady, but he held none of the squirming obsequiousness of most of her lackeys.

She did not turn around or move her gaze from the window. "Sir Kenneth, I think we might have a problem again."

"Marm?"

"You have been good to me over the years. Loyal. You have not asked questions."

"It has never been my place, marm."

"But have you not ever wondered? All the killings in France

in 1979? Then that troublesome woman in 1986? You carried out my instructions, yet not once did you ask the question why."

"I am your loyal subject, Your Majesty. I do as you bid. And besides…"

"Yes, Sir Kenneth?"

"I believe a secret should be a secret, Your Majesty."

"Quite." She went quiet. A bird in one of the trees seemed to be preoccupying her. She still did not look at him. Then she said, "I have been foolish, Sir Kenneth."

He came over and stood next to her chair. He also faced the garden. It was as if they were both having a conversation with the window.

"I should be the only one who knows the secret," continued the lady. "I should be taking it to my grave with me. But a few years ago, I was foolish. In a moment of weakness… I told someone. I told them something that no one but I should ever know. She has not mentioned it since, not in ten years. But now I am nearing the end of my life, I cannot take the chance that the secret will be known after I am gone. *That cannot be allowed to happen*. I deeply fear that there has to be one more death before mine. Do you think you will be able to take care of it for me again, Sir Kenneth? *Lord* Kenneth?" Now she looked up at him.

He did not look down at her. But he said, "As you command, Your Majesty."

Highgrove, Buckinghamshire, England

At the same time as Sir Kenneth Dean left the bedroom of the Queen Mother, and fifty kilometres to the north, His Royal Highness Prince Charles Philip Arthur George, Prince of Wales, Knight of the Garter, Knight of the Thistle, Knight Grand Cross of the Order of the Bath, Knight of the Order of Australia, Companion of the Queen's Service Order, Privy Counsellor, Aide-de-Camp, Earl of Chester, Duke of Cornwall, Duke of

Rothesay, Earl of Carrick, Baron of Renfrew, Lord of the Isles, Prince Great Steward of Scotland and eldest son of Queen Elizabeth II, was contemplating two reflections.

One was his reflection in the window of his downstairs drawing room here in Highgrove House. He saw the future King of England, dressed casually by his standards in green corduroy trousers, hideous beige check shirt and – of course – a brown tie. He was shorter than people imagined, only 175 centimetres. Not as tall as his idol, beloved mentor and great-uncle Louis Mountbatten – but everything else about him was an impression of, a tribute to, the man he wished had been his real father, the man murdered by the Irish on August 27 1979. It was the imitation of the Mountbatten regalness, the demeanour, even the vague what-a-bore-it-is-to-make-my-muscles-move-to-talk way of speaking, that gave Charles his stature not his height.

The second reflection he was contemplating was not visual but mental. He had been separated from his hysterical, suicidal, unstable, whore of a wife for nearly five years now, and divorced for one. But she would just not go away. She had been stripped of her royal status and outcast by the court. If he had his way, she would be outcast from the country too – exiled, like Uncle David. But of course, exile was for royalty and she was no longer royal. And he could not deny her access to the boys, not in this day and age. Time was, a King could solve all his problems with just a word…

Things had gone from bad to worse since the divorce. He had never expected (but he had hoped) that Diana would retire somewhere with the pension he gave her, play the dutiful 'Mother of the Princes' and fade quietly out of the public gaze. But he had not expected what had happened. The full public exposure of her betrayal, the Bashir interview – the listing of her lovers, both marital and post-marital. Even a rugby player, in the name of God! Grandma always said one should confine one's affairs to one's own class. But these weren't affairs. It was just sex, deliberately cuckolding him over and over, again and again and again.

But now she had gone too far. She was fucking another *Muslim*, for Christ's sake. The mother of the future King of England, the future Head of the Church of England, had her second consecutive Muslim lover. Diana had been with him since they had managed to persuade Khan that his health would be better served by ending his relationship with her. She had jumped from one to the next without pause, and Charles' 'People' had been watching them every step of the way.

Four weeks was a short time for one of her flings. But the more the Muslim got his feet under her bed (Charles sniffed in irony), the harder it would be to get rid of him. And the longer it went on, the more chance there was of Diana falling in love with him like she had with Khan and many of the others. She was fickle. She might even *make* herself fall in love with him, just to defy everybody...

Behind Charles stood the man who had been shown into the room fifteen minutes ago. The chunky, unshaven, rough-neck known as John Smith looked uncomfortable in the suit and tie he was wearing. It was not his real name, of course – but there were some things even the next King of England did not need to know. 'John Smith' would adequately suffice for the man who was the Head of 'Charles' People', the man who was the most ruthless, cold, callous and intelligent object the Special Boat Service had ever produced.

What he had to tell Charles had knocked the wind right out of the Prince's sails. Silly really, thought Charles, it was only the natural consequence of what had happened already – he should have expected it. But the spouse was always the last to know, whether he was King or pauper.

Emad 'Dodi' Fayed was going to ask Diana to marry him.

Well, that just could not be allowed to happen.

The princes could not have a stepfather – especially a

playboy Muslim stepfather.

Had it been just that, it would not have been an insurmountable problem. Money would not have worked, not with the Fayeds. But other methods of persuasion had been effective on others in the past. He was sure Emad and his father were considerate of their health – especially if, say, an inherited peerage was offered to the father ('services to shopkeeping').

But it was not just the proposal of marriage. John Smith had imparted other news, gathered from phone taps and other listening devices on the Fayed boats and at their properties worldwide.

Charles turned from the window. "And there can be no mistake? No doubt?"

John Smith shrugged and spoke with his London accent. "There's always room for doubt, sir. Especially where – er – these things are concerned. But there is no doubt about the information as gathered. Done by our own fair hands."

"But this cannot be. It is just untenable. It cannot happen."

"I believe it already has, sir."

"Unbelievable," Charles said again. He looked confused. "She – she must have done it deliberately. There is no need for these things to happen, not in this day and age."

"She always was a wilful little girl," said the third person in the room, dragging on a cigarette. "A stupid child."

"But *pregnant?*" pleaded Charles. "And by a Muslim? It – it cannot be. Something must be done."

"Yes sir," said John Smith.

"The question is *what?*" Charles looked towards the third person for guidance.

She took another drag on her *Dunhill*. She looked at him through the smoke.

"What do royals always do?" asked Camilla.

Boulevard Exelmans, Paris, France

Ron Becker was stark naked when his girlfriend arrived home at 22:30. It was not directly intentional, but sometimes Serendipity smiled on mere mortals. He had just showered and was drying himself in the salon while watching English football highlights on the TV when he heard her key in the lock. By the time she had entered the salon, he was standing there facing the door, towel over his shoulders and outstretched, flashing his goods at her, an inane grin on his face.

Gisele Joudeh seemed less than impressed. She chose to ignore his exposed dick which, it has to be said, with its south facing inclination seemed to be ignoring her also.

"So this is what you get up to when I am on lates!" she frowned, her French perfect but with the hint of a Middle Eastern accent. "Watching football!" she smiled.

Becker let the towel fall and she came over and embraced him. "Hello Princess," he said warmly in English, his London accent just the acceptable side of cockney. "Didn't think I'd start without you, did you?"

"*Con*," she said affectionately as she went into the kitchen.

Theirs was that sort of relationship, two strong but disparate personalities. He the short, stocky Cultural Affairs attaché at the British Embassy – where he had been stationed for the last twenty years. She the slender, classy PA to the Head of the Immigration Section at the Lebanese Embassy, six months into a two year tour of duty.

They had met at 'an embassy do' four months previously and had hit it off instantly, a fortysomething male and a thirtysomething female alone in Paris. She had moved in with him three weeks later, into his seen-better-days apartment in the Boulevard Exelmans in the nevertheless still desirable 16th Arrondisement. It was a move of convenience for both of them: he needed help with a recent savage rise in the rent, and she said she wanted somewhere with more comforts than the small garret in Malakoff. And the sex helped as well, of course.

They were a strange and unlikely couple – but often that is the best combination for a successful relationship. They were both fluent in several languages, but she steadfastly refused to speak to him in anything other than French, and he refused to speak to her in anything other than English. Naturally they both understood each other perfectly, but they got some strange looks in shops and restaurants.

Ron strolled into the kitchen as she prepared a snack of salami and that morning's bread. "Chelsea scored three times today," he held the fridge door open for her. "Do you think I will?"

"That is all you English think about!" she complained, but there was minx in her voice. "Football and sex! What is it with you barbarians? Anything to do with balls! Are you so base?" She removed some duck pâté from the fridge.

South facing Mister Willie (or Monsieur Guillaume) heard the conversation and began to take an interest.

"Straight and true, us Brits. At least you know where you stand with us."

"I know only too well where you stand – mind your *verge* in the door!" She closed the fridge. "*Imbécile!* Look at it! Pointing at me! That is disgusting. Still," she reflected, "if it is here it might as well make itself useful."

She scraped some of the smooth pâté onto her knife, grabbed him in her left hand, and spread the pâté over the helmet.

"Now," she said, satisfied. "That is much more pleasing to a hungry lady."

She was about to close her mouth over the end of his penis when the telephone rang.

"Ron Becker."

There was the smallest of pauses before a very familiar voice said, "Hello, Ron. It's been a while."

Becker's face dropped. "Mr Dean? I'm sorry, it's Sir Kenneth now, isn't it?"

"How are things over there in France?" asked the smooth, deep voice.

"As usual, sir. There's always some problem or - "

"Ron, I need your help again."

"You do?" He looked down at Gisele, who was continuing with her meal. The pâté was cold.

"We do."

"I see. Do we need to meet?"

"This time that would be... inadvisable. You remember the gentleman who assisted us before?"

"Yes."

"It is a job for him. For the same reasons as before."

The damn secret that must be hidden at all costs. Becker did not let Sir Kenneth hear his sigh. "I understand."

"I will send details in tomorrow's pouch. As quickly as possible, Ron."

"O-okay, sir."

"Is everything all right, Ron? You sound distant."

"Well, considering I'm having pâté sucked off my knob by a French-speaking Lebanese diplomat, I'm not too bad at all," he said to himself. Out loud he said, "It's not the best connection, sir."

"I can leave it with you then."

"As always, sir."

Ω

Wednesday 13 August 1997

Faubourg St Honoré, Paris, France

The Diplomatic Pouch arrived at 16:00 that day, the same time as it did every day. It used to come by plane, nowadays it came on the 09:50 *Eurostar*.

In his office on the plush first floor of the British Embassy, Ron Becker received the plain manila A4 envelope at 16:23. His name was written on the front, nothing else.

The envelope felt very thin considering it contained instructions for a hit. Usually there were full biographical details, family history etc.

Neatly he ran a carved wooden paper knife across the sealed flap. Inside there was just one item, no covering note. It fell out, face down, onto Becker's desk. He pulled the flap of the envelope wide, upended it and shook it in case there was anything stuck inside. There wasn't.

Casually he turned the item over, wondering who the unlucky bastard was this time.

The shock made him stand up involuntarily. His chair fell backwards onto the thick light blue carpet with a muffled *whump* and he grabbed hold of the desk to stop himself falling.

He stared at the item on his desk. They had to be kidding, of course. He gave a little nervous laugh. Then he grabbed the envelope and looked at his name on the front to make certain he hadn't been given something that was meant for the Press Office. Then he shook the envelope again, but it was empty.

They must be joking.

It was a photograph of Diana, Princess of Wales.

Ω

Thursday August 14 1997

Sarasota, Florida, USA

Ilich Ramirov could not help but appreciate the irony of the situation.

Ilych Ramirez Sanchez – Carlos The Jackal – had always been fictional. A cover character invented when the world's press became aware that there was just one co-ordinating and unifying force behind the global terrorist atrocities in the nineteen-seventies. Ilich Ramirov was, and always had been, a Major in the *Komitet Gosudarstvennoi Bezopasnasti*, the KGB. Cast off by his Russian masters on the fall of the USSR, he became a freelance. For a while he lived in freedom in Venezuela, foraging into the northern hemisphere when his special talents were required. He had gained a certain perverse respectability and was employed as necessary by governments and royal households.

After his arrest in Sudan in 1994, the deal with the French had been simple: he would not go to jail. They would let him go or papers he had left in discrete safety deposit boxes around the world would be released. These papers gave an audit trail of proof of the French government's involvement in the SAC (*Société d'Action Civile*) and the Order of the Solar Temple, and in the 'disposals' of many 'enemies of the Republic' (including the Domenici and Markovic affairs) which still continue in France today. If he was to die in French custody, the papers would be released also.

So he had been switched on the plane taking him to Paris. His double – a brainwashed stoolpigeon who thought his family in Venezuela would live in luxury forever more (paid for by the French) – was substituted.

On arrival in Paris, Ramirov had simply stayed in the WC of the plane until party and prisoner had left and then, dressed as a cleaner, he had disappeared into the night.

The French got what they wanted: the capture of the most famous terrorist in the world. He got what he wanted: continued freedom. His activities were, of course, severely curtailed (he was supposed to be in prison, after all) but that suited him perfectly. He was less than happy with the way things were going in world terrorism – there seemed to be just one fundamentalist cause now, a cause his Russian Communist heart did not agree with (the tens of thousands of his fellow countrymen killed in Afghanistan still rankled with him) – and his 'capture' gave the perfect excuse for the retirement of Ilych Ramirez Sanchez.

Ilich Ramirov Martinez, on the other hand could continue with his freelance activities. Right now, the irony was that if 'Carlos The Jackal' was dead, he could release the papers he had on the French and blow their cosy, selfish, murdering little Gallic world sky-high.

The French knew that, and in an official panic they had issued a statement that it was not Carlos The Jackal that had been found dead ten days ago, but his cell mate (a cell mate in solitary confinement!). Carlos lived, they said, and would face trial for his sins sometime in the future.

Yeh, right.

That morning, Ramirov shopped at Casa Italia on Constitution Boulevard as he did twice a week, exchanging pleasantries with proprietors Raj and Nita, and left with his wine (*Prunotto Barolo*) and imported *caciotta al tartuffo* (cheese with truffles) at 10:15.

At 10:55, after two more errands, he pulled into the driveway of his house on Sweetmeadow Circle, garaged the Ford Maverick and settled down with his coffee and that day's *Sarasota Herald Tribune* out on his lanai at 11:10. It was a hot Floridian summer's day, and he would not be able to spend too long outside.

He removed the cosmetic contact lens from his blind right eye and laid it on the table. He read better without it.

At 11:20 the fax machine in his downstairs office suddenly came to life with a whine.

Ramirov inclined his head and frowned. His normally accurate sixth sense had not given him any forewarning of this (although his scarred right shoulder had been aching more than usual recently). The only faxes he received were redirected on a circuitous route from the number in Venezuela via Tokyo, Mumbai, Vienna and Vancouver. Irritated, he neatly folded his paper, placed it on the poolside table and walked back into his house.

His irritation was soon assuaged.

The first thing to come out of the fax machine was a copy of a bank credit transfer advice confirming the transfer of five million US dollars into one of his thirty-one bank accounts (the one at the Bank Melli Iran in Dubai). He raised his eyebrows, and his mess of a blind eye began to water. His terms were a fifty per cent pre-payment, so someone was paying for something big.

He picked up the credit transfer advice to let the next item come out of the machine smoothly.

The machine seemed to tease him as the paper came out oh so slowly. The print head was on overtime. He saw the beginnings of a photograph. The top of someone's head began to appear. *Was that a tiara?*

And then he began to laugh. And laugh. And laugh. They had to be joking!

In the name of Christ and Allah, another one of them! He thought back to 1986 and shook his head. Did they want him to kill all the females of that stupid family?!

Ramirov did not know that halfway across the world, the fax that he was at that moment holding in his hand was about to make two other people laugh too. This time it was a laugh not of amusement, but of triumph.

Via Catalana, Rome, Italy

It had taken them five days.

Five days of cruising the world from the small apartment on the Via Catalana. Five days that had started off in awe, fascination and delight from Christina, but which soon turned to shock, horror and downright fear as the implications of Barking Dog had been brought home to her in graphic detail.

Every network, every website in the world was open to them. Every computer could be accessed *even if that computer was not turned on*. Providing it was plugged into an electrical source and was connected to a telephone line, it was theirs.

Just on a sample basis they had randomly accessed the computer of two schoolteachers in Riverside, California (they now knew everything about Charles and Tracy Slaughter, their two kids Charles Junior and Sara, their financial status, everything – even the fact that they were ardent Dodgers supporters); then they chose a Reserve Army Captain and his family in Canberra, Australia (Ben Digan had a weekend off from active service and was going to visit his granddad Bob); and a school for handicapped children in India (Asha Niketan in Bhopal run by Irish nuns, Sisters Christopher and Philomena).

The power at the Israelis' fingertips was endless – and the implications terrifying.

In their hunt for Ramirov, Melanie and Christina had started with the obvious: his name, and all conceivable versions of it.

There were thousands of hits on 'Carlos The Jackal' and 'Ilych Ramirez Sanchez', but not one on 'Ramirov'.

They had then played what they thought was their trump card: Ramirov's DNA. But trump it did not. There was not one match in the world.

Then they had tried various forms of interrogation regarding people with one eye. There were over two million hits on the internet alone.

It was then that Melanie suggested they let The Professor make all the enquiries and collate all the information for them.

Who the hell? "The Professor?" queried Christina.

Melanie explained that it was another Mossad resource. A small country like Israel with limited universal intelligence resources needed all the technological assistance it could get. The Professor, a facility emanating from Tel Aviv, could do the work of two thousand human minds – at once.

Ramirov was just one thing. Whether it be terrorism for his original Soviet masters or his latter occupation as freelance advisor and assassin, he was, simply, a hired gun. The Professor would collate and analyse data concerning all international terrorist events and high profile deaths since… they put in 1974… to see if there were any links or trends.

The only snag was, The Professor would keep wanting answers to questions. It needed to be told directions to go in. Which meant that either Christina or Melanie would need to be at or near the computer at all times.

The women had taken it in turns, three hours on, three hours off.

For five days.

After three days, The Professor reported six events where 'someone had got away', either in fact or rumour:

1) THE ATTEMPTED KIDNAPPING OF THE BRITISH PRINCESS ANNE IN 1974 (RUMOUR).
2) THE MURDER OF LOUIS MOUNTBATTEN BY THE

IRISH IN 1979 (FACT).
3) THE ASSASSINATION ATTEMPT ON POPE JOHN PAUL II IN 1981 (FACT).
4) THE DEATH OF PRINCESS GRACE OF MONACO IN 1982 (RUMOUR).
5) THE DEATH OF THE DUCHESS OF WINDSOR IN PARIS IN 1986 (RUMOUR).
6) THE BOMBING OF THE WORLD TRADE CENTRE IN NEW YORK IN 1993 (FACT).

The Professor asked for further refinement. The women went for the majority involvement in the list: the British.

The Professor accepted the further instruction – and went quiet for two days.

As Melanie prepared dinner that afternoon and Christina sat reading a thriller by the up-coming American writer Harlen Coben, the computer gave one small electronic beep. The Professor was reporting back.

"Mel!" Christina called. She was wary of touching the machine.

The red-haired Brit came in, wiping her hands on a tea towel. "What have we got?" She sat next to Christina on the couch and pressed two buttons on the laptop.

1) 1974. KIDNAP OF PRINCESS ANNE, LONDON. FAILED.
2) 1979. MURDER OF LOUIS MOUNTBATTEN, SLIGO, IRELAND. SUCCEEDED.
3) 1986. DEATH OF DUCHESS OF WINDSOR, PARIS. SUCCEEDED.

LINKS:
A) ALL MEMBERS OF BRITISH ROYAL FAMILY (QUERY ACCURACY 1986);
B) EVENTS CARRIED NO KNOWN ADVANTAGE FOR ANY GROUP (QUERY 1979);
C) ALL SINGULAR PERSONS;
D) POSSIBLE STOOL PIGEONS ARRESTED FOR 1974 AND 1979. 1986 CONSIDERED NATURAL BUT MANY WEBSITES QUERY THIS;

E) PERPETRATORS KNOWN TO HAVE BEEN CONTACTED BY FAX.

UNUSUAL FAXES:
1) NSA RECORDS SHOW ONE FAX SENT FROM BRITISH EMBASSY DUBLIN TO NUMBER IN VENEZUELA TWO WEEKS BEFORE 1979 EVENT;
2) NSA RECORDS SHOW ONE FAX SENT FROM BRITISH EMBASSY PARIS TO NUMBER IN VENEZUELA TWO WEEKS BEFORE 1986 EVENT.

That was the end of the analysis. Melanie pressed 'Page Down' but the screen did not move.

"NSA?" queried Christina.

"National Security Agency," explained Melanie. "American."

Then another page popped up on the screen.

FURTHER INFORMATION:
FAX SENT FROM BRITISH EMBASSY PARIS ON AUGUST 11 1997 AT 19:00 HOURS TO SAME NUMBER IN VENEZUELA. ATTEMPTING TO OBTAIN COPY.

Both women were quiet. "Oh my God," said Melanie softly. "I think this is it."

"It can obtain a copy of a sent fax?" Christina was astonished.

"It piggy-backs onto the American Echelon satellite surveillance system. You didn't think faxes, e-mails and phone calls were secure, did you?"

"Well, I neffer thought," Christina shrugged.

"They listen to and read everything. Wait! Here it is."

Up popped another screen showing the top half of a fax sheet. It was a bank credit slip, a little indistinct because of all its electronic incarnations, but showing a deposit of five million US dollars into a bank account.

Melanie scrolled down. The second half of the first page came into view, and then in slid the second sheet of the fax.

They frowned. What was that?

They both realised at the same moment that it was upside down, and they both turned their heads sideways.

It was a neck wearing a necklace. Then came the chin, then –

They looked at each other aghast.

"Does this mean what I think it meanz?" asked Christina.

"Even The Professor can't tell us that. He links, he informs," explained Melanie. Then she said, "And it looks like he has just informed us that our man has been contracted to kill Princess Diana!"

PART THREE

Ω

PROGRESSION

Ω

Friday August 15 1997

Rue de la Pompe, Paris, France

Veronique Chevalier had never worked in her life. She had never needed to. She had been born into money. Daddy had been a bigwig *advocat*, rising to become a Chief Prosecutor in the Interior Ministry or something – she didn't really know and she didn't really care. He had kept her and Mummy very 'comfortable' at their country estate near la Ferté-Alais in Essonne. She was his only child (although there were rumours of a bastard daughter somewhere, a mistake with one of his mistresses), and she had been spoilt since birth.

She had married Michel Chevalier seventeen years ago. She had married him at Mummy and Daddy's behest. She had been twenty-five and had had numerous 'fiancés', and Mummy and Daddy had thought it best that she 'settle down'. And she would do anything to please Mummy and Daddy, because the only thing she loved more than them was their money.

Michel Chevalier had simply been her fuck friend at the time. He too was in law, a divorce lawyer, and nowadays he was away a lot – but that did not matter because Veronique was proud of the fact that not even for one of her seventeen married years had she been faithful to him. And poor Michel knew nothing of her infidelities, he was an unknowing serial cuckold.

Perversely, Mummy and Daddy had died four days after her and Michel's engagement. Murdered in 1979. But Veronique had inherited everything and, to please their ghosts, she had gone ahead with the marriage to the hapless Michel anyway.

Today Michel was away (again), and that afternoon she had spent four hours being pleasured by Didier, her black stud from Marseille. So at 18:00 that evening she had a warm, contented glow to go with her bruised inner thighs, twinging rectum and still damp and swollen sex.

When her 'gentlemen friends' visited, she always gave the maid the afternoon and evening off, so she was alone in the apartment in Rue de la Pompe when the doorbell rang.

Still glowing with thoughts of Didier, she walked across the large hallway and opened the door.

"*Bonjour.*" The person standing in the doorway was a jolly, fresh-faced woman in her thirties, brown hair cut in a bob around her un-made-up but nevertheless pretty face. She wore a knee-length pink floral dress which seemed un peu too loose on her. She carried no bag – something only a woman would notice, as Veronique surely did.

"*Bonsoir?*" Veronique allowed the one word to carry her query.

"My name is Charlotte Fleury. I'm from Apartment 16," explained the caller. That explained her lack of bag. "Three down and sort of two across."

Veronique smiled. The building on Rue de la Pompe was one of the more internally-complicated of the 1980's apartment blocks of the 16th. "How can I help you, Madame – er - "

"Charlotte."

" - Charlotte."

"The concierge gave me your name, I hope you don't mind."

"The concierge - ? Look, *excusez-moi*, please, won't you come in Charlotte?"

"Thank you."

"My name is Veronique."

"I know."

Veronique led the way into the salon, a bright modern room

with huge windows and an admirable view eastwards.

"Would you like a coffee? Or an aperitif perhaps?"

"*Merci.*" Charlotte shook her head. "I'm sorry to disturb you. You must think it a bit of a cheek - "

"*Pas du tout.* What can I do for you?"

"I was chatting to the concierge and I mentioned the trouble I was having with my ex-husband – I asked him not to let him in if he ever turns up here again, that sort of thing, you know. And he said I should consult a lawyer, about a divorce. He said that Monsieur Chevalier was a lawyer…?"

"*Ah, je comprends.* Please, sit down." Veronique indicated an ivory leather armchair to the left. "Are you sure you won't have a drink?"

"You are very kind," Charlotte smoothed her dress beneath her as she sat down. "*Oui. D'accord.* I will. *Café, s'il vous plait.*"

"I have some on." Veronique left the salon, turning left in the hallway.

Alone, Charlotte gazed out of the window. She could see the top of the Tour Eiffel above the Palais de Chaillot, beyond the older buildings over on Avenue Paul Doumer. She could actually make out the people up on the top floor of the tower, the *troisieme étage*, where Eiffel had his little apartment.

"*Et voila,*" Veronique came back in carrying a silver tray which she set down on the central glass table. There were 2 cups, spoons, a sugar bowl and a large silver coffee pot. Charlotte turned back from the window.

"So you will be divorcing your husband?" asked Veronique as she poured.

"I have no choice," explained Charlotte. "The man is a *bâtard.*"

"Aren't all men?" Veronique sat down in a matching leather chair, facing her guest.

Charlotte frowned and smiled at the same time. "But you are married."

"So? Men have their uses, true. But I am so glad Michel is,

what shall we say, *un mari du weekend*. If we were together all of the time I would have killed him long ago!"

Both women laughed.

"Can't live with them…" began Charlotte.

"…can't live without them!" finished Veronique. She was warming to her neighbour. "So Charlotte, you want my husband's advice regarding your divorce?"

"I know it's a bit of a cheek, me calling on you like this - "

"*Pas du tout.*"

"Is he here, your husband?"

"*Non*, he is up in Normandy until Friday." (Thank God, said her nether regions.)

"I thought we could do things amicably."

Veronique gave a rueful hmph. "There is no such thing as an amicable divorce, my dear. No matter what anyone tells you."

Charlotte put down her cup. "Don't I know that. I was married once, for a short while, a long time ago."

Veronique nodded. "So this is your second marriage?"

"No, once bitten and all that. I am finished with men. No one comes close to your first man, don't you agree?"

Veronique frowned. "I am sorry. I am confused."

"No, no, it is I who should apologise. When I said we could do things amicably I meant you and me."

Veronique just shook her head in puzzlement.

Charlotte stood up, picking up one of the small coffee spoons as she did so. "I should explain. I have entered your apartment under false pretences, and for that I apologise. But it was better than trying to explain my real purpose to you standing in your doorway."

"I'm sorry? *Je regret - *"

"Oh there's nothing to regret. I hope…" Charlotte was standing next to the older woman, looking down at the top of her expensively-styled head. Veronique looked up.

"You are Veronique Lensens, correct?" asked Charlotte.

"*Je m'appelle Veronique Chevalier.*"

"I don't care what you are called now. You were born Lensens, *oui?*"

"I don't understand, what is it you want? Not a divorce?" Absentmindedly Veronique was twisting her cup around between her hands.

"You are Veronique Lensens," continued Charlotte. "Your father was Chief Prosecutor Robert Lensens. He was murdered eighteen years ago, along with your mother."

Shock showed on Veronique's face. "What have my parents to do with you? I don't understand. In fact, I think I would like you to leave please."

Without warning, Charlotte's right hand slapped savagely across Veronique's face, knocking her head to the right. Veronique gasped, her hand going to her cheek.

"Shut up. I am talking," Charlotte's voice was cold. "Let us do this amicably. Just tell me what I want to know and I am out of here."

A small needle-thin trickle of blood appeared from the left side of Veronique's mouth. She started to get up but a surprisingly strong hand on her shoulder held her in the seat.

Charlotte bent forward and spoke into her right ear. "Your father was murdered because he knew something."

"My father was murdered by that thieving scum Mesrine - "

The hand shot to her throat, nails pulling the skin and digging into the flesh so tight that blood instantly appeared. "THAT IS A LIE!" snarled Charlotte. "A damn, damn lie that has been perpetrated for eighteen years! Your father was not murdered by Mesrine, he was murdered by the British." She squeezed the older woman's throat.

Veronique tried to speak but only a croak came out. Her face was turning maroon.

"You want to talk to me, huh?" said Charlotte as she eased the pressure. "That is good. You are a good girl."

"My... my..." Veronique was fighting to get her breath and speak at the same time. "My father was murdered by Mes - "

"NO, NO, NO!" Her head was slammed into the back of the chair again and again and again. The cup fell from her grasp, spilling coffee dregs onto the carpet. "You stupid woman! That is what they wanted you to think. So that they could hunt him down and murder him with justification. It was THE BRITISH that murdered your parents. They killed your father for what he knew. Can't you understand?"

Veronique's face was screwed up with fear and pain. Charlotte kept her hand where it was, silently staring at the other woman. Then she let go, leaving five distinct bloody finger marks dented around the neck. Veronique gasped for her breath.

"I know it is hard for you," Charlotte's voice sounded quite sympathetic. "To be told the truth about your parents' death after all these years. But you had to find out sometime."

Veronique continued to gasp, unable to speak even if she wanted to.

"Now," continued Charlotte, as if chatting to a friend. "Just to clarify. Jacques Mesrine wanted a document. A document containing a secret. A secret which the British wanted to repress at all costs. Your father possessed the document and kindly gave it to Mesrine. But your father knew the contents of the document. Therefore the British killed him. And shortly this led to the death of Mesrine also." Just for a moment Charlotte's voice caught in her throat as memories of her father flashed into her mind. Then she said, "And I think you know the contents of the document too."

Veronique was totally dumbfounded. She looked bewildered, scared, in pain and confused all at once. Blood was trickling down her chin. She was thinking back over the years. To her meeting with Mesrine. To his sexual violation of her, the most erotic experience of her life as his tongue poked between the cheeks of her bottom... To the contents of the document.

"What is it?" Charlotte's simple question snapped her out of her reverie.

Veronique looked up, rubbing her neck "What is what?" she asked softly.

"The British secret. The secret our fathers were murdered for. What is it?"

Veronique was now totally subdued. "I don't know," she mumbled.

"That is not the answer I want. I know you know." Curiously, Charlotte was looking intently at the silver coffee spoon in her hand. She spoke to it. "Just tell me, that's all. We can still be friends."

"All – all I know is that it concerned the British Queen. There was some agreement…"

"Think, *mon amour*, think. I beg you." Spoon in hand, Charlotte stared intently into the seated woman's eyes.

"I – I was young. I did not care. It – it was part of Daddy's collection. I wasn't interested."

"THINK!"

The shout made Veronique jump. A lady-fart popped from her bottom. She began to sob. "S – something about the Germans, Hitler and the Russian guy, I don't know. I DON'T KNOW! The Americans also…"

Charlotte was studying her face. "If I gave you time, would you remember more?"

"I…"

"Are you telling me everything? Sweet, sweet Veronique, are you telling me all?" Tenderly she stroked the other woman's hair.

"Please… I can give you money - "

The hand that had been tenderly stroking suddenly grabbed the hair painfully. "Money? MONEY? You think that is what this is all about? MONEY?" She pulled Veronique's head from side to side as she spoke. "You stupid, deluded, spoilt, selfish little bitch. This is about my father. This is about righting wrongs. I'll teach you about money - "

Charlotte's hand moved from the top of Veronique's head, to

cover her eyes and pinch her nose at the same time. Veronique opened her mouth to scream. Charlotte pushed the head backwards and rammed the spoon into the open mouth. Both lips were sliced and immediately blood gushed out.

The spoon was pushed into the mouth sideways, rammed further and further back, into the throat. Veronique gurgled and tried to breathe in croaked, jumping gasps. She tried to close her jaws around the hand in her mouth, but her muscles had frozen. Her face began to turn from maroon to blue. Her hands pulled futilely at the other woman's arms.

Charlotte removed her hand. Veronique thrashed around on the chair like a mute marionette, legs kicking, her own hands grasping at her throat, trying to get into her mouth. Charlotte could see the spoon wedged sideways, pushing the skin of her neck outwards at both sides.

"I will not kill you," Charlotte spoke conversationally, avoiding the thrashing legs. "Let the ghosts of our fathers decide whether you join them or not." But she already knew the answer. Veronique's movements were slowing, her eyes were gaping, and her own nails had stopped digging into her own neck. She sat slumped in the chair, just an erratic, occasional jumping gasp getting air into the body.

Then the jumping gasps stopped completely, and the glazed eyes went dull. A damp patch appeared in her groin area.

Veronique Lensens died as she had been born. With a silver spoon in her mouth.

It was at that moment that the front door opened.

Sarasota, Florida, USA

Six hours behind time-wise, but at the same moment that the front door of the Chevaliers' apartment opened in Paris, Ilich Ramirov sat in the hot tub on his lanai and let the full-power jets massage his body. It was a hot and humid afternoon.

The chubby, boyish face smiled. Some might think that killing the most famous woman in the world was the toughest contract he had ever been given. But they would be wrong – so, so wrong. This was the easiest contract ever, and he was being paid ten million for it!

It was easy precisely because of the fact that she was the most famous woman in the world. He did not have to find her! At any given time, he could establish her whereabouts just by turning on the television or consulting the internet. That very day he knew she was flying to the Greek Islands with her friend, the *Tiffany* woman.

It was just a matter of when and where.

And how.

The British would want it to look 'natural', like they always did – therefore there could be no assassin's bullet from the rooftops, no point blank shooting or knifing in a crowd. But the definition of 'natural' was broad. Wallis Simpson had stopped breathing and had died a 'natural death'. The death of French President Georges Pompidou many years ago had been a 'natural death', the cyanide gas inflicted by Ramirov had been untraceable. Car crashes were 'natural', like the ones he had organised for Princess Grace and the police sergeant lover of his current target – and the one he had arranged for the toff James Hewitt which had been called off at the very last possible moment.

Choking could be 'natural'. Food poisoning could be 'natural'. Even a fall could be 'natural'. The possibilities were endless.

So he needed to play God. To decide which 'natural death' he would inflict on Diana.

With the skills of Ilich Ramirov, she could die 'naturally' anywhere. He would do it quickly, the British would like that. What was their expression? 'No sooner said than done.' They had said, now Diana would be done.

In preparation for action, he would now relax. Have a little fun...

Play God.

He looked across at the person sharing the hot tub with him: Candice, the fat black prostitute with the sagging tits and stretch-marked belly whom he had picked up on the Keys an hour previously. She was drugged up and smiling at him sleepily but lasciviously.

He raised his right foot and pinched her left nipple between his toes. Her areola was so big, it spread either side of his foot.

Her body had been washed clean by the water, but there were still crusty stains around her mouth where he had already used her.

"Again?" she asked. "My, someone is a horny boy. The fourth one costs extra."

"An extra thousand bucks for something special." He used his Texas accent. Flawless.

"What would you like? An extra thousand gets you whatever you want."

"Whatever?"

"Whatever."

He stood up in the tub, his massive (and impressive) erection rising up from the water like a surface to air missile. She smiled in admiration.

He moved towards her face and she opened her mouth in anticipation, closing her eyes. His dick touched her lips but went no further.

Suddenly there was a downward pressure on her head. *What the fuck?* She went under, the water gushing into her open mouth. Her eyes opened but they were stung by the water. She couldn't see. The water had instantly filled her lungs. She couldn't breath.

She began to thrash wildly, trying to get his hands off the top of her head. Her feet pressed against the bottom of the tub, trying to push herself upwards, but she moved not one inch against the pressure on her head.

She gasped again, but nothing happened, no air entered her body. Now her arms began to jump erratically, up and down, above and below the water. Splashing, splashing.

She wanted to scream but no sound came out. Her knees now buckled and she felt herself sinking further.

The pressure in her lungs was hurting, hurting, hurting. Her head was about to explode. He was killing her!

The roaring started in her ears…

Suddenly there was air, and she felt herself lifted by her hair out of the water. She was gasping and choking at the same time, small amounts of beautiful, beautiful air entering her lungs and being expelled in small, harsh gasps.

He grabbed her shoulders and span her around, forcing her to bend from the waist over the edge of the tub. She thought he was going to try the classic manoeuvre to expel the water from her lungs. But instead, as she lay over the side gasping for air, gasping for life, she felt his hands on her butt cheeks as he forced himself into her.

"Whatever?" he mocked.

Rue de la Pompe, Paris, France

Charlotte took her eyes off the body of Veronique Lensens and span round to face the hallway as she heard the front door opening. She had no time for surprise, no time for fear, no time even to swear. She had to act on pure instinct.

Lightly she skipped out into the hall. A man was just closing the front door behind him. The suit, tie, slightly receding hair and weak almost craven-looking face meant he could only be a lawyer.

"Michel," she said it as a statement, not a question, as she came towards him.

He frowned, confused. "*Bonj – *"

"I wasn't expecting you until the weekend." Charlotte

jumped on tip-toe and her lips came up hard on his in a savage, drool-filled kiss. Her hands reached round and rubbed the back of his head firmly as her tongue poked into his mouth.

Being a man, Michel did not ask questions. He simply responded, his smoky breath forcing its way down her throat.

After thirty more seconds, she pulled away. Both their mouths and jaws were wet. She held his head in her hands, staring into his eyes. With firm, lust-fuelled sincerity she said, "I want you."

She grabbed his cock, which was solid beneath the suit pants. Then she moved her hand back up, and with both hands pressed hard on his shoulders, encouraging him down.

When he was kneeling on the floor in front of her, she raised her dress. She wore nothing underneath.

Michel gasped as he looked at her clean-shaven sex. He came very slightly in his pants.

"Kiss me," she ordered. "I want to feel your tongue."

Before he had chance to utter argument or thanks, she stepped towards him and rammed his head into her groin. Her hands held him there with surprising strength. She felt his tongue seeking for access.

She took one hand away from the back of his head, found the rim of her dress and pulled it down over his head.

To distract him, she moved her legs apart two centimetres to reward his probing.

Then, with the front of the dress over his head, she grabbed the rim in both hands and suddenly pulled herself away from him (shit, the bastard had one of her lips in his mouth!). She stepped round behind him.

Michel was kneeling on the floor with her dress completely over his head. She had the hem tight around his throat and was strangling him. She pulled harder and harder as she moved her left hand down over his face and pinched his nose.

He struggled but only weakly, thinking he was having the most bizarre, wonderful sex of his life with a complete stranger.

Only when he realised he could not open his mouth to compensate for his pinched nose did he think maybe the sex game was going wrong. And by then it was too late.

As blackness overcame him and his lungs screamed, he ejaculated ferociously. He wondered what Veronique, his precious, wonderful, faithful Veronique, would say if she ever found out about this infidelity…

Ω

Saturday August 16 1997

Henri's Bar, Paris, France

Only *Le Figaro* made the connection. The other newspapers reported the deaths as straightforward murders, and they left the story for the inside pages. But Le Figaro topped them all.

HISTORY REPEATS

Socialite and husband murdered in bizarre family coincidence

Chief Inspector Pierre Jamo casually glanced at the story as he ate his morning croissant at the zinc of the bar at the corner of Rue de Penthièvre and Rue Cambacérès, opposite the back entrance to the Interior Ministry building. He went to open the paper, but then a word from the front page caught his eye and he closed the paper back up again, frowning curiously.

Had he seen what he thought he had seen? Where was it? Was his mind playing tricks?

He scanned the lesser articles on the page, especially the ones on the right near where he had been holding the paper. Then he looked again at the main story, his eyes moving up and down the columns. At first he could not find it, so instead of scanning he read the article in detail.

And there it was.

And he did not believe it.

He could not believe it. It was bizarre, as the paper said.

More bizarre than even the editor of *Le Figaro* knew. But *coincidence?* No, coincidences were not pack animals. Coincidences despised each other. There was never more than one of them in the same place at the same time.

He sighed and pulled his chunky mobile telephone from his pocket. He went through the palaver of extending the aerial and got into his memory at the third attempt. He highlighted the wrong number, pressed green before he realised and then quickly pressed red. *Oh for God's sake, these bloody things.*

"*Henri! Jetons, s'il te plait.*" He threw some francs down onto the counter as the elderly proprietor gave him the tokens for the telephone on the wall near the WC.

The old telephone had a dial, it was not even push button, and he connected in one attempt. It rang three times before she answered.

"*Oui?*"

"Inspector, I need you immediately."

"But I'm on lates today, I'm not in until - "

"Now. You have fifteen minutes."

"Fuck you."

"Not on duty, I have told you that before."

"Can't you - ?"

"Now."

Jamo hung up. He had never been to her apartment in the north of the city, their occasional medicinal fucks (done for mutual relief, no emotions involved) had always taken place at his place in Montparnasse. But he knew it would take her thirty minutes maximum to get in. Just enough time for him to finish his croissant.

And just enough time for him to start worrying what the hell was going on.

Rue des Saussaies, Paris, France

Inspector Claudette Ibrahim had a face on when she entered the BCP suite twenty-seven minutes later. She was dressed in her usual riding gear of T shirt, leathers and boots, and she had managed to apply some make-up (daytime eyeshadow and lipstick), but she was as pissed as hell for being called on duty a full five hours before her shift.

Jamo knew better than to try any pleasantries when she was in one of her moods, so he went straight into it.

"Have you seen the papers?"

"I haven't had time. Some bastard disturbed my morning." She thumped her red crash helmet down on her desk.

"Seen this?" Jamo tossed the folded *Le Figaro* over to land next to the helmet.

She looked at it and feigned astonishment. "Why, what is this?" The sarcasm could have been cut with a knife. "It looks like – what? What is it? Parchment?" She picked it up and felt it carefully. "No! No, it's paper! And what is this black stuff on it, it is coming off on my hand." She sat on the edge of her desk and began to remove her boots. She looked with a sneer at Jamo. "Which is more than certain people will be doing."

"Shut it."

She gave the main article a quick scan, mood satiated. She asked, "What is it? No political involvement, is there? The murder of a socialite and her husband." She pulled a pair of denim jeans from a rucksack, and slipped her leather trousers down.

"Read it carefully."

She did. Meanwhile Jamo enjoyed the view of her white G-string pants, the string actually invisible between her cheeks. He felt jealous.

Five seconds later she stiffened. "They're joking."

"I don't think so."

She read aloud as she pulled up the denims. *"Socialite Veronique Chevalier and her husband, society lawyer Michel Chevalier, have been found murdered in their apartment in Rue de la Pompe* – very nice. *Veronique, thirty-seven* – yeah, and the rest – blah-di-blah-blah... *Loving husband Michel... responsible for handling the divorces of many high society* wankers – blah-di-blah. *In a bizarre twist of fate, the parents of Madame Chevalier – Chief Public Prosecutor Robert Lensens and his wife Rosemary – were murdered together eighteen years ago by Jacques Mesrine. Monsieur Lensens was the Chief Prosecutor responsible for jailing Mesrine for twenty years, and he was killed in an apparent act of revenge just nine days before Mesrine himself was shot as he was being recaptured."*

She lowered the paper slowly and looked across at the Chief Inspector. She said lowly, "Mesrine."

Jamo nodded. "Mesrine. Dead for nearly two decades, and now suddenly he's back. Our former Chief screams his name down the telephone before he dies in flames. Four days later a woman whose parents were murdered by Mesrine while he was involved with us is herself murdered along with her husband."

"How did they die?" Claudette raised the paper back up.

"Doesn't say. 'Thought to have been strangled' - "

"But the police are not releasing details at this time... Strange."

"Unusual, yes. But you know what this means, don't you?"

"I think I can guess."

"We can no longer leave it to the PJ. Somehow we – the BCP – are linked to this. But we have to find out. Why was Charles Fleury-Goujon killed? And why now? And why were Veronique Chevalier née Lensens and her husband killed? And how? And why now?"

"And," said Inspector Claudette Ibrahim, "who else is going to be killed?"

"And," said Chief Inspector Pierre Jamo, "why?"

They paused, Claudette giggling to herself at the dramatic moment. Then she said, "You know something, Chief?"

"Quoi?"

"You should have called me in earlier."

Sarasota, Florida, USA

Ian Ramsey, the first generation Texan of Scottish parents, left the house in Sweetmeadow Circle at 10:00. Ramsey was a man of medium height, long blonde wavy hair tied in a simple but smart ponytail at the back, complemented by a blonde goatee on his face.

He was a rich man whose money had come from oil (as any internet check would confirm), and he now lived off his investments.

His round face made him look a tad paunchy and overweight, a condition not helped by the loose beige linen shirt worn over the baggy multi-pocketed cargo pants. It was a perfect illusion which hid the tough, muscular and powerful body underneath.

Ramsey threw his back-pack into the trunk and climbed into the pre-booked taxi. Exchanging not one word with the driver, they set off for Sarasota-Bradenton Airport and his connecting flight before the long journey eastwards.

Ω

Monday August 18 1997

Athens, Greece

Ian Ramsey landed at Eleftherios Venezelos Airport, Athens, at 06:30.

It was four years before the seachange of September 11 2001 so, although immigration checks were made in accordance with the laid down procedures of the time, the Greek authorities did not check the names of arrivals against the passenger manifest of the arriving airplane.

Thus it was that the Texan Ian Ramsey left the USA on August 16 using his legitimate American passport, and the Greek Ioannis Rigakis presented himself at immigration at Athens using his equally legitimate Greek passport.

A cursory customs check of the returning national's one item of baggage revealed just clothing, shaving items, two books and sundry knick-knacks purchased in the USA and well below his duty free allowance limit.

No comment was made about the hand-wide, six centimetre deep tin of shaving soap in amongst the toiletries, and it was not even touched let alone opened.

Ioannis Rigakis reached the port of Piraeus at 10:30 hours.

Rue des Saussaies, Paris, France

"So run this by me again," Commissaire Gillian Colet stared hard at Chief Inspector Pierre Jamo, who stood before her like an errant schoolboy in front of his principal. Colet had that affect on men: if they were needed to advance her career, she was the coquette. If they were not needed to advance her career, she was a hard faced man hater.

A piece of her permanently-up-during-office-hours long grey hair had fallen down and it moved back and forth against her left ear. "An old man is murdered," she said. "He may or may not have screamed Mesrine at you down the telephone on the day he died. Four days later, a wealthy socialite and her husband are murdered. Eighteen years ago, *eighteen years*, this woman's parents were murdered by Jacques Mesrine. And you think there's a link. A link of which you have no proof, just supposition. And you want the BCP to take on an investigation of both murders."

"Yes."

"Why?"

"Charles Fleury-Goujon was our first, our original, Commissaire - "

"Need I remind you what the BCP is? What we do? We are the Bureau de la Co-Operation Politique. We are responsible for the protection of, liaison with and the general comfort and happiness of all foreign government interests in France."

"Yes, I do know that." Jamo's face showed no emotion.

"We do not investigate murders. That is for the *Police Judiciare*."

"I have a feeling that the murder of Fleury links straight back to the days he sat in this office."

"Proof?"

"Until I investigate, I have no proof."

"But we do not investigate murders."

"You know the rumours that Mesrine was connected to this office. That he was working for Richer and Fleury."

"That is all, Chief Inspector." Already she had picked up some papers from her In Tray.

"You're a fucking cow, you know. An incompetent salop who fucked her way into her job," mumbled Jamo as he walked back down the corridor to his office.

Claudette Ibrahim knew the answer as soon as he slammed through the door. "I take it that's a 'No' then."

"The bitch didn't even want to listen."

"I knew she wouldn't. I could have told you. I *did* tell you."

"*Oui, d'accord, d'accord.* Don't rub it in." He patted his pocket for his cigarettes.

"You know what your problem is?"

"Oh, here we go. Upward management again."

She came over and stood beside him. "Your problem," she reached forward and put her hands on either side of his face, "is that you are too nice."

"You didn't say that the other night when I was ripping you apart inside."

"Shut it. Your problem is that you have to do things 'the proper way'. Mister Missionary." She shook his head gently. "Why do you have to go through her anyway?"

"She *is* the boss," he said through puckered lips as she pushed either side of his face inward.

"She is the *bitch*." Claudette leant forward and pecked him on his protruding lips, then she let go. "I know, I know," she said as she went back to her desk. "I understand. You are the Chief Inspector, the chain of command *et cetera*. So we let it drop."

Jamo looked shocked. "Did I say that?"

Claudette looked up.

"Do you really think I'm going to let that bitch, who has never been on the beat in her life, tell me what to do?" asked Jamo. "The woman whose only qualification for office are that she fucks indiscriminately, men and women, whoever it takes to further her career? No way, Inspector, no way. We investigate. I hereby make it official. Let the PJ faff around, they don't know what we know. You and I will look into it from our angle."

"She'll have your balls." But Claudette was pleased.

"She will not. Currently my balls are in your court."

"Oh yes, you're right. I think I saw them in my drawer here..."

"Inspector!"

"Yes, Chief?"

"Remember the chain of command."

"Yes, Chief."

"I have it in my apartment. It has eighteen links, remember?"

"I know, Chief."

"How many did we manage?"

"Seven in the front and three in the back, Chief."

Jamo grinned. "Want to try for eight and four later?"

Le Marais, Paris, France

Les escargots are a cliché. Foreigners, especially those from the Anglo world, really think that those and frogs' legs are the staple diets of the French. In fact, a majority of French do not like either.

But Chief Inspector Pierre Jamo was not in the majority. He tucked into his plate of 16 snails swimming in garlic butter and relished every dripping mouthful.

Opposite him in the little restaurant in the Marais sat Eli Lucas, his oldest friend and, coincidentally, Chief Crime Reporter for *France Dimanche*.

Although controlled by the administrative unit called the *Sûreté*, the five police forces of France are effectively independent. Pride and jealousy are rife among the forces, and their dislike of one another is such that not only would it be unthinkable that they would co-operate with each other or give mutual assistance, but any request for help or information could well be met with disinformation or downright lies.

So there was never any question of Pierre Jamo asking for the co-operation of the *Police Judiciaire*. Instead, as in the past, he got his information from a much more trustworthy source: the French Press.

"It is strange, strange, strange." With his black hair and black moustache, Eli had more than a touch of the Mediterranean about him. He spoke through mouthfuls of steak tartare, blood from his raw mince staining the corners of his mouth. "Veronique Chevalier suffocated to death on a spoon."

"On a *what?*" A snail shell clicked back down onto Jamo's plate.

"A spoon," confirmed the journalist. "A coffee spoon. It was found wedged in her throat. They had to slit her throat on the post mortem to get it out. A cutlery caesarean!"

Jamo grimaced at his friend's graveyard humour. "So they are sure it was murder? Not some bizarre suicide?"

Eli chomped on a piece of pink-stained lettuce. "What do you think, *mon ami*? If you wanted to kill yourself, would you really go to all the trouble of ramming a spoon down your own throat?"

"Probably not."

"And your poor rich husband is so overcome when he arrives home and finds you that he puts some textile over his head, jerks off in his trousers and then suffocates himself to death. And then, just for good measure, his ghost disposes of the instrument of death before the bodies are found."

"They have no idea what was used?"

"He suffocated for sure. Fibres were found on his head and in his lungs. Cotton, dyed. But from what, they do not know. Likeliest theory is that it was a sack or a cushion or something."

"And what about this thing about Mesrine, the fact that he murdered both her parents - "

"Allegedly."

" – all those years ago." Jamo poured more Merlot into their glasses.

"There's no connection. Just a happenstance. But we're running a 'Poor Veronique Lensens' piece on Sunday. Showing how some lives are just cursed – parents murdered by Mesrine, eighteen years on daughter and husband murdered by intruders. The place was ransacked, don't forget. There was no money or jewellery left in the house." Eli picked up his glass and washed down his steak.

"No other connection?" asked Jamo.

"With Mesrine? How could there be? Dear Jacques has been pushing up daisies for nearly two decades."

Montmartre, Paris, France

Thinking back over the demise of Michel Chevalier, she couldn't help but smile. Men. What stupid, dick-driven creatures they were. One hint of sex and they would do anything – even let you kill them.

She snuggled her face into the sensuous fur of Will The Cat, who rested contentedly in her arms as she looked out of her window onto the vista of Paris below. Summer rain had cast a grey pall over the city.

"They are so, so naughty, my baby," she spoke softly into the cat's ear. "Why won't they tell me? I know they know. Is this secret so precious that they will all die for it? Surely not. Nothing is worth dying for. Daddy always told me that. Nothing."

She squeezed the cat and gently rocked from side to side, a little pout on her lips. For a while she was quiet. Then she made up her mind. She became business-like. "Right," she lowered the cat to her waist level and let it jump the rest of the way.

She went over to the bureau and opened a drawer, pulling out a manila folder. She placed it on her glass coffee table and sat down on her leather couch.

"Time," she said, "for the next one."

She opened the folder.

Ω

Tuesday August 19 1997

Largo Febo, Rome, Italy

A glorious Roman evening. The oppressive thirty-six degree heat of the day had waned to an acceptably hot twenty-six by 22:00.

Melanie Nathanson and Christina Cascianis sat at a table on the raised piazza outside the *Santa Lucia* restaurant and attracted admiring glances from many of the men (with or without their own female companions) who passed by on their *passegiata* around Largo Febo, the small square next to the Piazza Navona. Music drifted out from the restaurant.

Both women were dressed smart-casual. Christina was in a plain but fetching blue cotton dress, which displayed her still-fabulous-at-fifty legs to their best advantage. Melanie was in a green vest-style knitted top and off-white linen trousers, a colour combination that complemented her shock of natural red hair and suntanned skin.

The men who admired them had but one thing on their minds (this was Italy, after all) – and who could blame them? But they would have been stunned into disbelieving shock had they known the truth: that these women were two Israeli agents plotting the death of the most famous terrorist of the twentieth century.

"So how do we play this?" Melanie twisted her *tagliolini alla puttanesca* onto her fork. "Before, with Stelios, we used all our resources to locate and arrange the target for him."

"And that did not work for Stelios, did it?" After twenty-three years Christina could talk about the love of her life dispassionately. She took another mouthful of her *farfalle alle vongole.*

"That was bad luck. Some meddling Dutch policeman."

"True. But when we found Ramirov in Khartoum, it wass my team that did it."

"Equally true. But this time there is only a team of two. Us."

"So what do you think we should do?" Christina sipped her Verdicchio.

"I suggest nothing."

"Nothing?"

"No knee-jerk. Not yet. It's a different game nowadays."

"A game…?"

"Life is a game, hun."

"You think so?"

"With the whole world trying to throw a double-six. It's only the lucky bastards who manage it."

Christina smiled as she finished her dish. "I thought I had thrown the double-six with Stelios. Obviously I wass not to be one of the lucky bastards."

"Perhaps the great Gamemaster has realised his error and is now repaying us."

Christina put her fork on her plate and sat back. "How?"

"Well, we can't bring Stelios back - "

Christina said nothing.

" – but we have been given another chance for vengeance. We've been given that chance through a technology that was not even dreamt of back in seventy-four. A technology that nobody yet knows exists today." Melanie sipped from her glass of Barolo. Opposite her, the Greek woman lit up a cheroot. "We have found out that Ramirov's current base could be Venezuela. And it seems he has been contracted by the British to do something concerning Princess Diana. Look - "

Melanie stood up, went over to a vacated table and picked up a copy of that day's *La Repubblica*. She threw it down onto their table as she sat back down. "The Press is besotted with her. Diana is on the front of every newspaper, every magazine in the world. Now that she's hitched up with this Dodi Fayed, the Press are like sharks in a feeding frenzy."

Christina removed the cheroot from her lips and blew out smoke. "So we concentrate on Lady Di, not on Ramirov?"

"In a way. She is not our problem. But he is. He is coming after her. Where Diana is, that's where – sometime soon – Ramirov will be. We will simply wait for him to turn up. Then he will be yours."

"And this time," Christina signalled for the waiter, "there will be no arrest."

The waiter appeared.

"*Due espresso*," ordered Christina.

The man turned and then Christina called him back. "Make them *doppio*."

Ω

Wednesday August 20 1997

Via Catalana, Rome, Italy

"He can't be serious," said Melanie as she looked at the screen and read Barking Dog's response to their latest query. "He wouldn't do such a thing, would he? Would the great Ilich Ramirov be so unprofessional as to announce himself this way? I can't believe it."

"Ah, but remember," reasoned Christina, sitting forward and looking at the results displayed. "He does not realise he iss being traced. He thinks we think he iss in jail in France, following the death-of-Carlos-no-it-isn't fiasco last month. He thinks the world still thinks Carlos has been caught. And except for *Mossad Aliyah Beth*, it does."

"And I suppose we must not forget he is a man. As arrogant as they all are."

Christina grinned. "A genetic gender arrogance that hass played right into our hands."

And there on the screen it was. Barking Dog had ascertained that a certain Ian Ramsey had boarded a flight at Sarasota-Bradenton Airport in Florida USA last Saturday, bound for New York. At New York, he had changed onto an Olympic Airways flight direct to Athens.

The flight had landed at 06:30 on Monday morning. Greek Immigration showed no arrival for Ian Ramsey, but it did show Ioannis Rigakis, a native Greek returning from the USA.

The Professor had then taken over on request, and had linked the trip to Europe with Princess Diana in one nanosecond: the Princess was just ending a short break cruising the Aegean with her friend Rosa Monckton.

"I really can't believe it," Melanie clapped her hands together. "The arrogance, you're right. The great Ilich Ramirov has made the classic textbook error. Has he forgotten everything he learnt at Novosibirsk? He is using aliases *but he is using his own initials!*"

Christina nodded at the irony. "And he does not know that our baby here," she caressed the laptop, "can follow hiss every recorded move. But it does mean one thing," she looked up at the red head. "He hass locked on to Lady Di. We've got to move. And fast."

Island of Hydra, Greece

The man had long, wavy blonde hair, tied in a neat ponytail, and a goateed, chubbyish face which had obviously enjoyed copious amounts of moisturiser and other attention over the years. And there was a trace – just a trace – of eye shadow. He was dressed in sandals, three-quarter length white cotton beach pants and just-the-right-side-of-garish orange flowered shirt.

He sat in the guest lounge of the Hotel Leto, sipping his Metaxa and Coke, minding his own business. He had spent the day in the busy port area of Hydra Town, just two minutes down the road, overhearing, choosing, selecting. Now he was waiting.

And he didn't have to wait too long.

Claude Dumoulin, thin, balding and carrying two camera cases, walked into the lounge five minutes later and picked Ponytail up on his gaydar instantly. He came over and sat in a chair at the next coffee table along and ordered a beer when the barman approached.

Claude tried to make it look casual, as if he had just spotted

Ponytail sitting there alone. He nodded. "Ciao."

"Ciao." Ponytail smiled with just a nano-hint of coyness. Was there a trace of invitation?

"You here on vacation?" Claude spoke in French.

"*Oui. Deux semaines.*" Ponytail was French too. Was that a southern accent? "*Toi?*"

Claude smiled. The instant familiarity augured well. "Working."

"Oh? What do you do?"

"I'm a photographer."

"Really? That's fascinating. Glamour? Fashion?"

"Press."

"Sorry?"

"I'm a Press photographer." The barman returned with his beer.

"You got some big celeb in town?" Ponytail was interested, but not too interested. His sipped his drink.

"None other than Lady Di herself. She's just left."

"Lady Di? She was *here?* Really?"

Claude looked around as if he was about to impart a secret. He leant forward.

"She was with a girlfriend, the Tiffany woman. Shame really, we wanted to catch her with her new boyfriend."

"We?"

"There's loads of us here – even The Rat. Diana's worth money."

"I love Diana, always have," said ponytail. "You work for an agency? Sygma? Gamma?"

"No, I'm freelance. Completely independent."

"What a fascinating life you must lead." Ponytail finished his drink and looked at Claude expectantly.

Claude took the hint. "Another?"

"I'd like that. But can we go some place?"

"Of course. How about we raid the minibar in my room?"

"Raiding," nodded Ponytail. "I like that."

Ω

Two hours later, Ian Ramsey quietly left Claude Dumoulin's room and made his way back to his own on the floor below.

When the police called in the morning he would be open and honest with them. Yes, he had gone back to Claude Dumoulin's room. They had had consensual sex for two hours, then he had gone back to his own room. Why were they asking?

Claude was *what?* Dead in the shower? Broken neck? Looked like he had slipped on something sticky on the floor of the shower cubicle?

Ponytail would be shy, almost embarrassed. The floor of the shower cubicle? That was one of the places he had come. You don't think Claude slipped on…?

The police would be grave, but in their hearts they would be thinking *fucking queers*, and it would be unlikely the investigation would be taken any further. After all, the deceased's passport, credit cards and copious amounts of drachma were in his wallet, untouched. Nobody heard any noise coming from the room. There were no signs of violence. It was an accidental, post homosexual coitus death. Happens.

And they would not even know that such a thing as Dumoulin's Press affiliation ID existed, let alone that it was missing.

Ω

Thursday August 21 1997

Whitcomb Street, London, England

John Smith, Head of 'Charles' People', sat at the small table by the door in the *Hand and Racquet* public house in Whitcomb Street, just off Leicester Square, and waited. A half full pint glass of Director's Bitter and the remains of a cheese and pickle sandwich were on the table in front of him.

No need for a suit today, he was wearing his black polo shirt and blue denims, and he felt much more comfortable for it. It was more *him*. He hated having to dress in 'shirt and tie' every time he went to see The Boss. What did a shirt and tie matter? Smith did not believe that 'Clothes maketh the man'; in his case, six years in the SBS, his daily two hour workout and his membership of MENSA, maketh *this* man.

But he had to keep The Boss happy. And that was why he was now sitting in this pub that had seen better days, waiting.

It had taken a full week for The Boss to make up his mind, and Smith's instructions had finally been given to him over the telephone that morning. The phone call had been vague – not only through circumspection because phone calls were not secure (even the word 'Squidgygate' made him cringe), but also because that was The Boss: vague. You had to second guess him, work out what he really wanted. And Smith knew what The Boss really wanted this time.

Smith was surprised at his orders. The Boss had been separated from his wife for five years, and was now divorced.

But he still kept a critical eye on her activities. He haunted her. Or was it her who haunted him? He was now with the one true love of his life, Camilla, and yet he could not shake off – or leave alone – the mother of his children.

Whatever. This time, to quote The Boss, she had 'gone too far'.

As usual, The Boss had procrastinated. But, in true regal style, he had taken counsel and he had decided what to do.

And it was John Smith's job to arrange it.

There were twelve people in the pub at 17:00, with more trickling in by the minute. At 17:05 the door opened and five more people came in: two couples and a man on his own. The man was wearing a light grey suit with an open necked white shirt underneath. He was of medium height, trim with close cut greying hair which gave away his military background.

The couples went to find a table, the man went directly to the bar. He looked around as his pint was being pulled, saw Smith and nodded.

The man was Jack Jones – a name as real as John Smith – and he was the head of the MI6 Royal Family Liaison Team, known around the corridors of Century House as 'Betty's Men'.

He came over with his pint.

"John."

"Jack."

"I got your message, thanks."

"Thanks for coming."

Jones sat down. "So what's going on that I shouldn't know about?"

Smith smiled. *Twat.* "The Boss has a problem. Wants it solved."

"And I can help how?" He took a large swig of his Stella Artois.

"Just a little info, Jack. The problem is nothing for you to worry about. That's my department."

"Does he want you to fix the next polo match again?"

"Nothing so serious. Al Fayed, the Harrods bloke."

"Yes?"

"Have you got a briefing pack?"

"I can get one. Six has been keeping an eye on him for quite some time, as you can imagine. Poor sod still thinks he'll be granted citizenship one day." Jones looked up at the door as a giggling group of twentysomething females entered.

"You got people on the inside?" asked Smith.

"Bound to. It'll be in the pack. Ouch, look at that."

Smith followed his gaze. He had already noticed the blonde with the stunning Amazon figure. "How soon can I have it?" he pressed.

Jones looked back at him. "Tomorrow. Shall I have it biked? This is official, I take it?"

"Don't bike it." Smith thought of what he had been ordered to do. There wasn't a fan big enough in the world to handle the shit that would be flying from this job. And not one turd of it was even to point in the direction of HRH. "I'll pick it up. St James's Park at ten?"

"Usual terms?"

"Of course."

"Fine."

Smith raised his glass and clinked the bottom of it against Jones' glass. "Thanks, Jack. You're a brick."

But Jones' eyes were already back on the blonde Amazon and in his mind he was already licking Stella out of her belly button.

Ω

Friday August 22 1997

St James's Park, London, England

This was a fine day in London, and John Smith was in St James's Park half an hour ahead of schedule. He sat on what was known in the business as 'Six's Bench', the fourth bench eastwards on the northern lakeside path after the bridge.

He let the warming-up-nicely rays of the sun caress his face as he sat reading his newspaper. If anybody had cared to look, they would have been surprised to see this rough-looking, and now unshaven, man reading *The Times*. He looked as if he would be more comfortable reading *The Sun*. But, of course, at that time *The Times* was bigger than *The Sun* (its conversion from broadsheet to tabloid was six years away), and therefore more useful for his purposes.

From the bag on his knees, he pulled a slice of old bread and began to break pieces off and throw them to the ducks on the lake. As usual, the mallards were in the majority. They were the yobs of the duck world, he thought. But streetwise and canny. Just like himself really.

A swan glided past, too sophisticated even to look in the ducks' direction. But not too snobby to catch the piece of bread Smith threw towards it. In Britain all swans are the property of the Monarch, and Smith gave a little nod of deference. "Morning marm."

He saw Jack Jones walking across the bridge at 09:58. The MI6 man was also carrying a copy of *The Times*.

They exchanged pleasantries like old friends, and Smith offered Jones the bag of bread. For five minutes they sat there feeding the ducks and exchanging pleasantries.

Had he got off with the Amazon last night? No chance. But he had pulled her friend, the small brown-haired one with glasses. He was seeing her on her own tonight.

Were Chelsea going to win the FA Cup? Gianlucca Vialli had done wonders with them this season.

When they both got up, bidding each other farewell. Jones went back over the bridge, Smith went north towards The Mall.

They each had each other's newspaper.

Inside the one carried by Jones was one thousand pounds.

Inside the one carried by Smith was a CD-ROM.

Back in his office in the St James's Palace complex, Smith wasted no time.

Computer booted, he inserted the disk. The machine took twenty seconds to find and start the right program to open it. And then up popped what he had paid for.

The MI6 file on the Fayeds was extensive *[in the coming years it would grow to such a size that it could not be fitted onto one disk, even in a zipped format. The file was code named Paget].* It traced the history of the Fayed family.

Mohamed Abdel Moneim Fayed was born in the Bakas neighbourhood of Alexandria in Egypt in 1929, eldest son of a primary school teacher. He married into the wealth of the Khashoggi family and was employed in the Khashoggi import business in Saudi Arabia. He became financial adviser to the Sultan of Brunei in 1966, and then he came to Britain in 1974. In 1979 he purchased The Ritz hotel in Paris, and in 1985, with his brother Ali, he purchased Harrods department store in London, after a bitter battle with Tiny Rowlands (a bloody fight which at one point included Mohamed's arrest). Then came the 'Cash for Questions' scandal when Mohamed was accused of offering money to Members of Parliament Neil Hamilton and Tim Smith to ask questions in the English Parliament.

The file explained the persistent refusal of successive British governments to grant Mohamed a British passport. Ah, thought Smith as he read the reasons, that had never been made public. Still a spiteful pettiness by the British though, considering the sorts they *did* give British passports to.

The file had details and plans of all the Fayed properties around the world, even of his yachts the *Cujo* and the recently-purchased twenty million dollar *Jonikal* [later to be renamed *Sokar*].

The dossier was fair and factual – as would be expected from Six itself, but perhaps not from the biased Betty's Men. And it provided no explanation whatsoever for the constant demonisation and mocking of Mohamed Al Fayed by the British establishment and the British Press.

But, although it was good background, this was not what John Smith was after.

At first he thought it was not there. But then he found it. A small *Word* document tucked deeply between the plans of the *Jonikal* and a 30-page dissertation on the life of Emad (Dodi) Fayed's current (you're a bit behind there lads) fiancée Kelly Fisher.

It was a list of names. People whom he could contact if he needed to.

For British Intelligence had an agent in every Fayed business, every Fayed building throughout the world. They were all regular employees of Fayed, and they were paid substantial, six-monthly retainers by MI6 for their irregular services: keeping a watchful eye here, passing on information gleaned there, taking the occasional photograph (British Intelligence was experimenting with hiding cameras in mobile telephones and key rings).

This was good, thought John Smith. Very good.

He would need to make at least one of these people an offer they simply could not refuse.

Via Catalana, Rome, Italy

"Chris, come look at this," called Melanie from the *soggiorno*. "I think I need your help."

The Greek woman came in, drying her hands on a tea towel. "What iss it?"

"I know we missed her in Greece," said Melanie. "But I asked Barking Dog to scan Hellenic police networks, just in case there was anything reported. And look."

Christina leant on her colleague's shoulders and balanced her chin on Melanie's thick red hair. On the screen was a list of police communications made in the last five days concerning Princess Diana. The index was in the women's selected language of English, but the source reports would naturally be in Greek.

"Here, sit down," Melanie stood up. "Can you have a look at the reports? There's only ten of them. Is the drying-up done?"

"It's finished." Christina passed across the tea towel as she sat down.

It took only three minutes for her to read the Greek reports. "Nothing significant. Just reports noting the arrival and departure of the boat at the islands. The Press are following them, but there has been no trouble." As Christina turned to get up, her hand brushed against the Enter key. The screen changed. "Oh shit," she gasped. "What haf I done?"

Melanie peered at the screen. "Don't worry. You've activated The Professor. He will look for any wider links between my original inputs – Diana and Greek islands. There'll be nothing there."

But Melanie was wrong. Within two minutes she was calling Christina back into the room. In the kitchen, coffee was brewing.

"Chris, The Professor has found something. One link. A death on the island of Hydra one day after Diana stopped there." Even Melanie thought this was stretching things. "That's a link?"

"Let me read the police report," said Christina.

Melanie clicked the on-screen link, and a new page appeared. Christina read it.

"A freelance Press photographer named... Claude Dumoulin – what sort of a name is that? Mr *Windmill?* – slipped and fell in hiss shower at the Leto Hotel. Broke hiss neck. No sign of theft or violence. An accident." She turned. "But Diana had left the day before. I don't understand. Iss The Professor trying too hard?"

Melanie shrugged. "He only does what he's programmed to do. He just reports. It's up to us to accept or reject the link. But I don't see how this... Hold on, hold on. We have no record of internal travel, but let's make some assumptions. We know Ramirov arrived in Athens on Monday. We have nothing since then, but we know he is after Princess Di. Di is cruising the islands. So naturally we assume he follows her – but it's hard to know where the boat will be going next. He can't quite catch up with her. Wherever she goes, he arrives there after her. She visits Hydra, he arrives there just after she leaves. Then the next day a Press photographer dies."

Christina nodded in understanding. "It iss hiss cover," she said it lowly, matter-of-factly. She was staring at the screen but her eyes were elsewhere, looking back twenty-three years. "He hass done it in the past. He assumes different identities." There was a small catch in her voice. "Mr Ramirov has become a Press photographer, a paparazzo."

"Time then," said Melanie, "for us to move. He's getting closer. And so are we. Log in to the Fayed websites. Find out where Diana is next. We need to be there."

Montparnasse, Paris, France

"So what do we have?" Chief Inspector Pierre Jamo sat at the small table in the kitchen of his apartment in Montparnasse and watched admiringly as Inspector Claudette Ibrahim cut sandwiches over on the work surface. Except for a dainty apron tied around her waist, she was completely naked. The small, shapely-but-rock-solid rump and muscular back were lightly tanned, without a bikini line.

"Salami and cheese," she turned, her taut breasts a perfect complement to the trim curves below.

"No, no, no – the case. Mesrine." Clarified Jamo as the plate was set down on the table and she turned back to get the pot of coffee.

"Work, work, work, that's all you ever think of!" she sighed in mock exasperation.

"Not always," he grinned.

"Sex, sex, sex, that's all you ever think of!"

"Inspector!"

"Sorry, Chief." She sat down and in her turn admired the hairy chest opposite her, above the hint-of-podgy stomach. There was a distinct bite mark above his right nipple.

"Mesrine. Let's go through it," Jamo folded a piece of loose salami and popped it in his mouth. "One, Commissaire Charles Fleury-Goujon."

"Charles Fleury-Goujon," said Claudette. "The original Commissaire of the BCP. Paralysed in a fire eighteen years ago in which two other men died. Officially it was a Masonic meeting. Unofficially, there are suggestions that it was a brotherhood far higher even than the masons."

"The Organisation. The OAS."

"*Oui*. Fleury and one of the two BCP Chief Inspectors at the time, Paul Richer, were involved in… what?" She paused to take a bite of sandwich. She spoke with her mouth full. "We do not know. Nothing has ever been proven. But it is thought it all goes back to Algeria in 1958. It is thought Paul Richer was a friend of Jacques Mesrine – a *flic* and the most infamous criminal this country has ever produced! It is all rumour, rumour, rumour. Speculation."

"So let's go both ways - "

"We already did half an hour ago. Have you forgotten already?"

"Stop it. Officially what do we have?"

She sipped her coffee. "Chief Inspector Paul Richer and Chief Inspector Claude Gerard were both involved in the final hunt for Mesrine. Gerard found him. Richer died apprehending Mesrine. Gerard was killed the next day."

"Not by Mesrine then."

"Maybe by his accomplices, his gang. Three days later, Fleury and two others were trapped in a fire at a Masonic stroke OAS meeting up in Belleville. The two others died, Fleury was paralysed."

"An accident?" Jamo picked up a sandwich and began to take out the salami and cheese.

"No proof otherwise. Faulty electrical wiring."

"Too many deaths an accident does not make."

She looked at him stone-faced. "Whatever. Tell me, was there any point in me making sandwiches if you are going to pick them apart?"

He finished his coffee and poured more into both their cups. "Unofficially?"

She watched him put the pot down and begin to eat the components of the dismantled sandwich. "In short, Mesrine was working on something for Richer and Fleury. They even helped him bust out of jail. Gerard just got in the way."

"Do we know what Mesrine was working on?"

"No."

"Do we know if he succeeded?"

"No."

"Don't know much, do you?"

"Fuck you, Jamo."

He gave a Cheshire cat grin.

"And don't even think about it," she warned. "Twice in one evening is enough."

"Who says?"

"Says the pussy you're poking. And as of ten minutes ago, we're on duty... sir."

"I like a subordinate who shows me respect."

"Its not only my respect I've shown you. For a Chief Inspector you do, surprisingly, have your uses."

"Is that all I am to you? A sex object?"

"Yes. Have I ever led you to believe otherwise?"

He looked at her tanned skin, the muscular shoulders, the pert small-nippled breasts. He said, "Move in with me."

Inwardly she winced. It was not that unexpected. Why did men always have to complicate things? She could have been cruel, but she let him down gently. "You know I can't. It's not allowed. We shouldn't even be fucking."

He sighed. "I know, I know. But it's a nice fantasy, *n'est-ce pas?*"

She said nothing.

Jamo sat back in the chair, running his hands down through his hair and over his face. "Do one thing for me, will you?" he asked with a touch of weariness.

"Chief?"

"Find out as much as you can. What was Mesrine working on? Who else was involved? How does Veronique Chevalier fit into all this. And why, eighteen years later, are people beginning to die again?"

Ω

Saturday August 23 1997

The South of France

The tall blonde woman in the striped pastel swimsuit screamed in fear and joy, and clung tightly to her companion as their jet-ski bounced over the Mediterranean Sea just off St Tropez.

The machine came to a stop and Diana swung her right leg over Dodi's shoulder, as if to emphasise his smaller stature.

They laughed. My, how they laughed.

They seemed oblivious to the army of photographers, snapping at them through 300mm lenses from the shore. Or others in small motor boats or on their own jet-skis coming as close as they dare, as close as Rees-Jones and the Fayed security boys, watching from the nearby *Jonikal*, would allow.

On the shore, paparazzo Claude Dumoulin trained his camera on the laughing couple. This Dumoulin was a chubby-looking man with a completely bald pate and a veritable forest of black hair poking out through his half-undone shirt. He was nodding gently, his head slightly inclined to the left, as he focussed on the happy woman with her leg in the air.

But there was no film in his camera. This was just pretence. If they had not wanted it to look natural, this would be a gun he was holding.

And right now her head would be splattered across the blue Mediterranean.

Fish food.

Ω

Sunday August 24 1997

Monte Carlo

From her position on the Place Beaumarchais, Christina watched the excited hoard of photographers clammering outside the Hotel Ermitage and Repossi's, the society jewellers. Diana and Dodi had arrived a few moments before.

She scanned the faces. None of them even looked remotely like Ramirov.

But she knew he would be around somewhere.

She could feel it in her bones.

But this was frustrating, waiting for him to show his hand – waiting for him to do whatever it was he was going to do to Lady Diana.

And what he was going to do was obvious: Ramirov wasn't a kidnapper, he was a killer. Diana was to be assassinated.

Christina and Melanie had discussed reporting the matter to 'The Authorities'. They had discussed it with Tel Aviv, and Tel Aviv had agreed with them: the murder of the English Princess was nothing to do with the Israelis. Their mission was the elimination of Ramirov. If they prevented the assassination, all well and good. Otherwise, tough.

The Fayed Camp in London were quietly leaking to the Press the couple's planned itineraries one or two days in advance. Barking Dog had latched on to the telephone calls and faxes from Max Clifford's office. So the Israelis knew that today was Monaco, tomorrow was Portofino (the one in Corsica). After that had not been decided.

And where Diana and Dodi would be, so would be the paparazzi. And in amongst the paparazzi somewhere, they knew, was the world's most notorious and ruthless killer. Waiting to strike.

Ω

Monday August 25 1997

Rue des Saussaies, Paris, France

"We must approach it logically," said Inspector Claudette Ibrahim. "eighteen years is a lot of ground to rake over. Things can be buried deeply over such a length of time. Mesrine has passed into legend and memories fade. So I think we should start from the present and work backwards...

"Commissaire Charles Fleury-Goujon is murdered. As he is dying he phones this office – you – and screams 'Mesrine'. Presumably his killer's name. But how can that be? Has Mesrine come back from the dead. *C'est impossible.*

"*Alors,* Veronique Chevalier née Lensens is murdered in a most horrific fashion, choked to death by a spoon wedged down her throat. To me that sounds like revenge or torture. Revenge for what? Torture for what?

"The first suspect in such cases is the spouse. But Michel Chevalier is murdered too. He could have murdered her before being murdered himself, of course – but that's stretching things. The chances are the same person killed them both. Who was the intended victim? Obviously Veronique, because of the manner of her death. The husband's death was more simple, a straight suffocation. He probably just happened to be there. So let's put him to one side.

"Charles Fleury-Goujon and Veronique Chevalier *née* Lensens. What is the connection between them? Why, it's none other than the late, lamented Jacques Mesrine. Mesrine stole some papers from Veronique's father eighteen years ago, and then four days later came back and murdered the father and his wife. Revenge on the Chief Prosecutor who put him away for twenty years.

"But wait a minute. Does this *really* make sense, looking back at it? Why didn't Mesrine kill Chief Prosecutor Lensens at the same time as he stole the documents? Why come back four days later to kill him?

"Let's make an outrageous assumption. Let's assume Mesrine did *not* kill the Chief Prosecutor, somebody else did. Similarly, let us assume that Mesrine's so-called 'gang' did not attempt to murder Charles Fleury-Goujon three days after Mesrine's death. Somebody else did. Where does that leave us with Mesrine?

"Mesrine is working for Chief Inspector Paul Richer and Commissaire Charles Fleury-Goujon of the BCP. He is searching for a document for them. He finds it, in the ownership of Chief Prosecutor Lensens. He takes it from him. Before Mesrine can deliver it to the BCP, he is shot while being re-arrested. Paul Richer dies at the same time. Let's just pause there..." She looked over at Jamo, who was rapt.

She went on. "Is it all logical? Does it all make sense? *Mais oui*. It is known Richer was chasing after Mesrine's car when he died. Was Mesrine about to hand over the document to him? No document was found in the car, in any of Mesrine's houses or boltholes, not on his tart Sylvie Jacquot, nowhere. So where was it?

"Now then, let's leave that story there. Let us treat what happens subsequently as a new story.

"The day after Mesrine and Richer die, Chief Inspector Claude Gerard – the *flic* responsible for locating Mesrine – is killed in Montmartre. Why and by whom? We have assumed it was revenge by Mesrine's 'gang'. Let's now assume nothing of the sort.

"Two days later, an attempt is made to obliterate the High Command of the OAS, of which Charles Fleury-Goujon is

Colonel-In-Chief. Fleury only just escapes with his life, but he is paralysed, finished. The others die.

"And then that is it. It all stops. *Finito.* So what unanswered questions do we have? Firstly, the document – where is it? What happened to it? What does it contain? Secondly, the murders of Lensens and Gerard and the attempted murder of Fleury. If we discount revenge, why were they murdered? What is the other main reason for murder? To keep people quiet. Why did Lensens, Gerard and the High Command of the OAS need to be kept quiet? Because they knew something. What? Where the document was? No. People would want to know that information, not have it kept quiet. So what did they know... What the document *contained?* Ah, ha! Now that is something someone might want kept quiet. Perhaps the document contained something that was worth killing for. Logical, *oui?*"

"*Oui,*" nodded Jamo.

"But after all this, it all goes quiet. Lensens and Gerard are dead, Fleury is effectively dead. The document has vanished, the contents suppressed.

"And it remains that way for eighteen years. Then, out of the blue, Fleury is murdered – really murdered this time, in a way that suggests torture. Veronique, the daughter of the last man known to possess the document except Mesrine, is tortured and murdered too.

"Both tortured. Torture is used to extract information. What information? What is the link? *Bien sûr*, the link is the document, not Mesrine. They both have knowledge. What knowledge? The secret of the document.

"Suddenly, eighteen years later, the secret rears its head again. And those who know it, or *might* know it, begin to die. Who has started the killing again?

"And" continued Inspector Claudette Ibrahim, "what the fuck is this secret that brings death in its wake down the generations?"

Ω

Tuesday August 26 1997

Rue des Saussaies, Paris, France

"Utter bullshit," commented Commissaire Gillian Colet the next day when Jamo quoted Ibrahim's theories to her almost verbatim. "Granted Inspector Ibrahim presents a very good case, a thesis that would have earned her goods marks at the Academy. But in the real world it is bullshit. And, as I have said before and you know I do not like to repeat myself, we do not investigate murders."

"*Mais - *"

"If she is so confident of her ideas, perhaps she should share them with the *Police Judiciaire*. And perhaps she should join them. The BCP has its own responsibilities. The new boy Prime Minister of England is visiting soon, and we need every available member of staff to ensure his comfort."

"But - "

"That is all. Please get back to your work. Your BCP work, Chief Inspector."

Jamo slammed his fist down onto a thick pile of folders on his desk. "That's the last time that bitch humiliates me."

"I told you not to even try," said Claudette. "You are a fool to yourself."

"That is all the thanks I get?"

"You will get your thanks in five days time, I've got the plumbers in at the moment."

"Great. Well, we're not giving up. We've got that new guy from England visiting soon, and Lady Diana keeps popping in with her latest lover, but apart from that the summer workload isn't too bad. The mundane stuff can be handled by the sergeants. So, Inspector - "

"Yes, Chief?"

"Clear the decks. We've got some murders to investigate. Commissaire Colet can go fuck herself. And when we've solved this, I'll take it straight to the Minister himself."

Henri's Bar, Paris, France

"So we are agreed. Mesrine is the secondary link," said Jamo. "The document – the secret – is the first. Someone again wants to know the secret. And they will go to extreme lengths, even murder, to find it."

Claudette nodded as she popped the last piece of croissant into her mouth. They were at the *zinc* in Henri's Bar.

"What we need to establish," mused Jamo as he took a swig of his *vin rouge*, "is who would know the secret? Other than those who want it suppressed. Paul Richer, Charles Fleury-Goujon, and perhaps Claude Gerard, all knew it – and they are all dead. Veronique Chevalier née Lensens might have known it – she might have seen it in her father's collection. Dead. *Alors*, who else might know it?"

"We must go back," Claudette gave Jamo a look as he lit a *Gitanes*, but said nothing about it. "Back eighteen years. Who is still alive who might know the secret? Whose life might we save if we get there before the murderer?"

"Who, if anybody, would Mesrine have trusted?"

They both looked at each other and said simultaneously, "Sylvie Jacquot."

Ω

Wednesday August 27 1997

Rue Ponceau, Paris, France

Professionally she now went by the name of Renée, in memory of her lover, her future husband, her life, which had been taken from her so cruelly on November 2 1979. The day France had murdered Jacques René Mesrine. She had been shot and wounded at the same time, and their child – Fifi, the poodle – had died in her arms at the scene.

Jacques had been her future. She had been the future Madame Mesrine. They had been on their way to start their new life in Marly-le-Roi, but God had decided that they would never get there. Not only that, but God had decided that she would be left destitute as well – for Jacques had not changed his will. Everything was left to his family – she was not even mentioned.

When she was thrown out of hospital after ten days, she had nowhere else to go. Their apartment in Rue Belliard was rented, and the lease had expired. Their new apartment in Marly-le-Roi now belonged to his family. So back she went to her old apartment in Rue Ponceau – and back to her old life.

And very soon she was as popular as ever.

But that had been eighteen years ago.

Now she was in her late middle forties. The hair was still bottle-assisted blonde and the breasts – always disproportionately huge and with an horizontal suspension that defied both gravity and science – had grown even bigger with age.

But she was a realist. Experience was always required, but so was fresh meat. A few years ago, when she finally admitted to herself that her 112HH bra had mysteriously become too small to contain the girls, she had decided to make the natural progression upwards. To a business of her own.

She did not run a house, that would be too grand and she would need a 'sponsor'. But her telephone agency had been popular from the start. Firstly by word of mouth from her clients both past and present and then – in the more liberal nineties – by discreetly worded advertisements in various suitable magazines.

It was a good living, and she still ran it from her apartment in Rue Ponceau. Real estate which in 20 years had changed from being regarded as in the downmarket, whore-lined Rue St Denis area to upmarket, sought-after 'Paris Centrale'.

The doorbell rang. That would be her 14:00 interview, the new girl. She went over to the entry-phone.

"*Allo?*"

"*Bonjour, c'est Veronique Lens madame.*"

"*Bonjour ma belle*, come on up. *Deuxième étage.*"

Renée made one final check in the mirror on her way to the front door. Not bad, she thought, for a woman with a lifetime of adventure behind her – and enough men to fill the Stade de France (several times over).

Veronique Lens was a slim girl, long blonde hair (looked more *l'Oréal* than peroxide), dressed in a pretty flowered dress and small pink jacket, carrying a small, strapless handbag. She wore only light make-up. Surprisingly, she was older than Renée expected. She looked to be in her early thirties.

After introductory pleasantries, including a kiss, Renée stepped aside and admired Veronique's bubble butt as she walked inside.

"*Café, ma belle?*"

"That would be nice, thank you." Veronique had a low, very pleasant voice.

The kitchen and salon were open plan, an 'American Kitchen' as the Europeans liked to call it, so they talked as Renée prepared the *Maison du Café*.

"Please, sit down if you wish Veronique."

"*Merci.*" She sat rather primly on the edge of the armchair, legs together, bag clasped on her lap. The timid, submissive type, thought Renée. A lot of men liked that.

"You are," Renée came straight to the point, "older than I imagined."

Veronique smiled politely. "Does that cause a problem, madame?"

"Call me Renée, please. No, no problem. My agency caters for all tastes." She came in with a cafetiere, then went back for the cups. "Have you done this work before?"

"No."

"Then why, may I ask...?" Renée brought in two mugs.

"I am divorced," Veronique sighed, noting that there were no spoons. "The bastard cut me off without a *sou*. He disappeared. No matter what the courts may decide, he cannot be found and maintenance orders cannot be enforced. I need money."

"There are easier ways," Renée sat down opposite her.

"Sugar?" asked Veronique.

"*Pardon?*"

"Do you have sugar?"

"*Ah, mais non. Je suis desolée.* I don't take it, and I never think to have it in for my guests."

"*Pas de problème. Du lait?*"

"Neither."

So no stirring necessary.

Veronique sipped her black coffee. She said, "Yes, there might be easier ways – for some. But for me? Non. I was married to that bastard from an early age. I have a certain lifestyle to maintain. A certain circle to move in. I cannot be seen working the till in Monoprix for ten hours a day!" She laughed. "And what could be easier than fucking? Minute for minute, the most profitable job around."

Renée was looking at her appraisingly. Her naïveté, her keenness, reminded her of herself when she first started out. She nodded. "I will need to train you, to ease you in."

"As you wish, madame – Renée."

"May I see you?"

"Pardon?"

Renée moved her hands, indicating Veronique's body.

"Ah," Veronique understood. She put her mug and bag on the coffee table. Business-like she stood up and removed her small jacket. Then she reached down to the hem of her dress and in one fluid motion pulled it off over her head and dropped it to the floor.

She wore nothing underneath save for her high-heeled shoes.

She stood there in front of the other woman.

Renée was impressed. "You shave?"

"Obviously. My husband liked the little girl look."

"So do many of my clients. It is also more hygienic. Turn please."

Slowly Veronique turned a full three-sixty.

Renée nodded in admiration. "You have a superb bottom, *ma belle.*"

"Thank you. So I've been told."

"Please, put your dress back on."

"Before I do, can I ask you something?"

"Bien sûr."

"Seeing as you've seen one of my little secrets," Veronique nodded downwards. "Could you tell me one of yours?"

"One of my secrets?" Renée laughed. *"Ma fille,* I have so many. We do in our profession. What subject would you like?"

The nude woman stood with her legs slightly apart, confident body language.

"I want to know *the* secret."

Renée frowned.

"The one Jacques died for."

It was as if Renée had been punched in the face. She was literally knocked back in the chair.

"Jacques…?"

"You are Sylvie Jacquot, are you not? His last lover - "

Renée was confused. "I – I was more than his lover. We were to be married."

"And they murdered him, I know."

Tears welled in the older woman's eyes. "He was my life. I had given up everything for him…" She looked up, frowning. "Who… Who are you?"

Veronique knelt down on the floor next to the chair. She took Sylvie's hands in hers. "You never met any of his family, did you? His children. He never introduced you."

"That – that was for the future. When we had settled in Marly." She could smell the gentle musk of the naked younger woman.

"But that was never to happen," said Veronique. "They had decided that. They killed him. But why?"

"Why?! He was Jacques Mesrine, the most wanted man in Europe."

"But was that reason to kill him?"

"What are you saying?"

"Have you never asked yourself why he was executed? Gunned down in the street like a wild dog. You lived with him. In those last months he was searching for something. For a secret. I know he found it. I want to know what the secret is."

Sylvie was crying, the newly reopened sores of her memories almost too much to bear. "I – I don't know. He never told me things. For my own good, he said. So I could never testify against him if he was re-arrested." She gave a sad, humourless laugh. "He always used to say 'What little girls don't know won't hurt me.'"

Veronique was gripping her hand tightly. "So you know nothing about the secret?"

"It was all to do with the Captain."

"The Captain?"

"From his army days. Captain Richer – how could I ever forget that name? 'For richer for poorer.' Jacques found whatever it was he was looking for. It was a letter or a document. To do with the British. He never let me see it. The day he was…. was…. he got me to post it to Richer. I never knew what it was." Her eyes had glazed with her memories. Her darling, darling Jacques. At that moment she wanted to die, to meet him in eternity.

Veronique just knelt there, holding Sylvie's hand, unconcerned with her nakedness.

Then Sylvie looked up. "And you are…?"

"I am a daughter out to avenge her father. A daughter seeking the truth. Seeking to know why. Seeking justice." She raised herself off her haunches. "Let me tell you about myself."

Leaning forward, she began to kiss Sylvie Jacquot on the mouth…

Sardinia

The boat *Iliad* bobbed up and down on the gentle Mediterranean waves, making it difficult for the ten men lined up against the port side to take a good picture. About two hundred metres in front of them sat the *Jonikal*.

But never mind. This was Diana and Dodi Fayed. This was the romance of the century: the Christian Virgin Bride and the Muslim Playboy. The world's papers and magazines were paying fortunes, even for blurred shots of the couple.

Claude Dumoulin was at the end of the line of clicking crows, at the bow of the boat. To maintain his cover he had to appear to be one of them - he had even chipped in his five thousand francs share to hire the *Iliad*. But he knew nothing would happen today. There were no 'natural deaths' he could arrange out here – short of pulling Diana over the side in the darkness, like he had done with Robert Maxwell six years before.

Dumoulin was just keeping up appearances being on the boat. But he was a very, very patient man. He had five million US dollars worth of patience.

His opportunity would come.

He looked up as a helicopter flew over his head.

It would be recorded later that the helicopter was hired by photographer James Andanson *[real name Jean Paul Gonin, and himself to be murdered in 2000]*. In fact the helicopter was hired by Israeli Intelligence. The reason it hovered above the *Jonikal* was not to get pictures of the yacht and its occupants, but so that the passenger in the helicopter – a woman with stunning red hair – could get pictures of the occupants of the *Iliad*.

Ω

Thursday August 28 1997

Sardinia

"Barking Dog has checked all of them," said Melanie back at the Cervo Hotel in Porto Cervo. "And guess what? They all check out – except one."

"Yess!" Christina punched the air. "It iss Ramirov, yess? Do we haf him?"

"Hold on, hold on. We *think* we have him. Barking Dog has determined that this one is not a photographer, but at the moment we don't know who the mystery man is. Barking Dog is checking the world's ID databases."

"Describe him."

"Bald, for a start. And I mean really bald, not shaved. Chubby face - "

"Good."

"One seven eight centimetres, huge belly, hairy chest and – would you believe? – wearing a medallion!"

"Hmm."

"The Americans have Facial Recognition Technology, and Barking Dog has cuckooed into it. We'll know soon."

Barking Dog reported back seventy-two minutes later.

Melanie looked at the screen.

"FRT has given us six matches. All passport applications. All the same person, but with a series of different names and looks.

Ibaldo Ronaldo, a Brazilian. Igor Rimski, a Russian. Ioannis Rigakis, a Greek. Ib Rahman, a Qatari. Ito Rennes, a Frenchman. And – ah here it is, hun – Ian Ramsey, a Texan." She sat back in the chair. "Mr Ramirov, you are ours."

"But haven't we forgotten something?" said Christina. "They've gone. The yacht has gone and the photographers have gone."

"I know"

"And we let them go."

"What were we supposed to do? Two middle aged women. Should we have gone to the gang of photographers and said sorry but please could you stay here in Sardinia until our computer identifies which one of you is not a photographer but an international assassin? It's no problem, Chris."

"You think not?"

"Ask yourself something. Why hasn't he done it already, Ramirov? Why hasn't he killed Diana?"

"I don't know."

"The Professor brought it to our attention. Princess Grace, the Duchess of Windsor. The Royals. Only *rumours* when it is the Royals. Why? Because the deaths seemed 'natural': a car crash, asphyxiation due to throat blockage in her sleep. Ramirov is planning a *natural* death for Diana. Something he cannot do at sea, unless he makes her fall overboard like he did with our agent Robert. He is waiting for his chance. And now we know where he will try it."

"We do? Where? How?"

"Their next itinerary has just been released. They are going to Paris for a night on Saturday."

Barking Dog provided the connection into all the world's databases. The Professor was the most powerful information link program yet devised. The systems were not prey to RiRo [*rubbish in, rubbish out*]. No human data input was required. The systems merely needed to be told what to do. They provided accurate information.

But then came the weakness. The information was provided to humans. It was up to the humans to interpret and analyse the results given.

And that was how, on August 28 1997, the Israelis made one huge, fundamental, glaring error.

Rue Ponceau, Paris, France

Inspector Claudette Ibrahim sat on her Ducati M900 outside 3 Rue Ponceau and looked up at the second floor windows through the open visor of her crash helmet. Her natural instinct to get things done, to get things sorted, was urging her to go and kick in the front door. However, her police training held her back. One unanswered cold call did not entitle her to force entry. Sylvie Jacquot might be out shopping. Or working.

Claudette wondered whether to leave her card in the letterbox, but she decided against it and started the bike.

As she drove off down Rue Ponceau and turned right into Rue de Palestro, she saw two local girls on the corner, dressed in the obligatory revealing outfits, doggies on leads, chatting in between clients.

Claudette smiled. No *salad basket* for you today ladies, feel free to continue your good work.

Rue des Saussaies, Paris, France

Claudette was back in the office when Jamo arrived at 15:00. He had spent the morning at the Vietnamese Embassy over in the 16th, mediating on a matter regarding a junior clerk at the embassy and certain sexual demands made by a senior consul.

"Good afternoon, Inspector."

"Afternoon, Chief."

"Any luck?"

"She wasn't in. I didn't leave my card."

"Best not to alert her. Don't want her running scared for no reason."

"The Bitch wants to see you."

"*Merde.* When did she call?"

"About an hour ago."

Jamo picked up the phone and keyed the Commissaire's number. "*Bonjour, salop.* Washed your fanny today?" He put the phone down. "She's engaged. I'll go along."

Commissaire Gillian Colet was off the telephone and was examining a folder on her desk, reading glasses on the end of her nose, when Jamo entered by invitation.

"Ah, Pierre. *Merci.*" She was being pleasant. Meant there was a job on.

"Commissaire," he nodded. She did not invite him to sit down.

"I've had the Minister on the phone. The British have contacted him. About Lady Di. You do know Lady Di?"

"Of course I do, you stupid bitch. She's only the most famous woman in the world." He actually said, "*Bien sûr.*"

"Apparently she's going to be popping in and out of France a lot. With her new beau, the Fayed boy. She was already in Paris last month, on 25th – but nobody except the Fayed security people knew about it. The embassy didn't know until afterwards."

"*Oui.*"

"The Brits cannot ask officially because Lady Di is no longer royal, and she has foregone official protection. But she does not know about the *unofficial* protection. They have asked that we look after her – discreetly – when she is here."

"I will need more staff."

"Which you cannot have. She spends a lot of time on the Fayed's yacht, so you can liaise with the local forces down on the coast. You have national jurisdiction, so there will be no problem."

"And here? The father owns The Ritz, does he not? And several other properties in the city."

"When she's here, you and Ibrahim look after her. No one else. It is unofficial, after all. When she is in the city, she takes priority over all other work. Understand?"

"Of course I understand."

She looked up at the edge in his voice.

"Do you know when she next plans to be here?" he asked.

"No. You find out."

"*D'accord.*"

"How were things with the Vietnamese?"

"Oh, apparently the junior clerk liked and welcomed the attention of the senior consul. The complaint was made by a nearby resident who could see their adventures from her window." He looked over at Colet's window and at her enviable view down Avenue de Marigny. "I told them to keep the blinds closed."

He turned, and as he neared the door the Commissaire said casually, "How are things with Mesrine?"

Jamo smiled to himself. He was used to her little management techniques. He turned. "This office has nothing to do with Mesrine."

She smiled triumphantly. "Good. Please remember that."

He turned to go and once more she called him back. "Pierre?"

"*Oui?*"

"You coming round tonight? It is appraisal week."

He thought of Claudette and her visiting plumbers. Might as well. "*D'accord,* Gillian," he said with a small smile.

"The Brits cannot ask officially because Lady Di is no longer royal, and she has foregone official protection," explained Jamo.

"I can accompany her while she is here," suggested Claudette.

"Oh yes, in your leathers and with your kick-the-door-in attitude, you'll make the perfect complement to her."

"I can be a lady when I want to be."

He smiled. "Don't I know that. No, we are to be discreet. She is not to know she is being protected."

"Disguise?"

"Maybe. We'll see. Liaise with the British, will you? See what they think, when she'll be here, *et cetera*."

"What about Sylvie?"

"I'll try to see her tonight."

Rue Ponceau, Paris, France

At 23:00 the streets were as busy as ever. Rue Ponceau might now be 'Paris Centrale' rather than the sordid 'Rue St Denis District', but the girls still plied their trade in the time-honoured fashion.

Business was brisk tonight, the girls were busy, and Jamo was propositioned only once as he drove slowly up to number 3. The girl thought he was stopping because of her waving, and she walked up business-like but sensual as he opened the door.

"Hello handsome. Care to party?" She wore a black basque with open-nippled brassiere, suspenders and black stockings. A small G-string covered her play area. A large silver-studded black leather bag was over her shoulder. She had no dog, therefore the bag would contain – amongst other things – a gun or a knife.

"Not tonight, LouLou," smiled Jamo.

The girl frowned. She liked to try to remember all her customers, but this one's face escaped her.

"And," continued Jamo, "I don't like boys."

"Ah," the prostitute nodded, and the voice that came out was now purely masculine. "Now I've placed you. How are you, Inspector? What's it been? A couple of years? Come to pull me?"

"In neither sense," said Jamo. "And it's Chief Inspector now, I've moved on to other things. I'm not Vice any more."

"So I'm a lucky girl then."

"Know if Renée's in?" Jamo looked up to the second floor. The curtains across the windows were heavy, but there were no telltale cracks of light.

"Haven't seen her for a couple of days. But there's no reason I should. She only employs bitches."

"Now, now, young man. Behave yourself. Just because nature gave you an unwanted dick."

LouLou grinned and turned her back. "Want to poke your nose into my business?" the feminine voice returned.

Jamo gave the naked cheeks a firm slap, and the hermaphrodite ran off giggling down the road.

A man was just leaving the building (flushed but sheepish) and Jamo caught the front door before it could close.

Up on the *deuxième étage* there was no reply when he pushed the bell button. He waited a few moments and then banged with his fist on the door. "Madame Renée!" he called.

Nothing.

Now this was worrying. Claudette had failed to gain entry yesterday. There had been just the ansaphone on for two days. And what nobody but Jamo, Claudette and the perpetrator knew was that Sylvie Jacquot was potentially the next victim.

Potentially? Or now actually?

Jamo pushed at the door. Naturally it did not budge. Tentatively he tried his shoulder against it. Painful. Where was Claudette and her one-kick-and-I'm-in when he needed her?

Okay, he would have a go. If she could do it, so could he.

He stepped back across the corridor.

"Monsieur?"

The query came just as he was about to take off. He looked to his left.

Coming up the stairs was a middle-aged woman, bottle-blonde hair, massive breasts straining the stitching on her flimsy summer top, nipples protruding a full two centimetres from the tits and stretching the garment even further.

"Madame Renée?" Jamo fought to gain his composure and at the same time not to stare at the incredible mammaries.

"*Oui.*"

"I wonder if I might have a word?"

"Who are you, monsieur?"

Wordlessly, in case of ears, Jamo produced his ID.

She glanced at it superficially and nodded, also silently. "Come in, please."

Her legs were clad in tight denim jeans, and she carried an overnight bag over her shoulder. Jamo nodded a mental *bonsoir* to her bottom as she passed.

Renée had washed and changed into a red dressing gown. She now prepared coffee in the kitchen as Jamo sat at the small table and admired the still-shapely middle-aged legs and, of course, the arse. He did not know that nineteen years previously Jacques Mesrine had sat at that same table and had the same thoughts about the woman as Jamo was having now. Carnality never changes.

Coffee made, Renée came over with the pot. Bowls and a basket of rolls and croissants were already on the table. At Jamo's querying look when she had first set them out, she had said "It is never too late – or too early – for breakfast, m'sieur. I eat when I want to, I eat when I need to. Join me if you wish."

Now Jamo broke a roll and dipped it into his coffee, enjoying the illicit feeling of breakfasting at midnight – and with a Madame as well.

"So, m'sieur," Renée was sitting at ninety degrees to Jamo, to his right, giving him an admirable view of her assets as the dressing gown dropped open at the cleavage and leg. "Which one was it?"

"Which one was what, madame?"

"The word you wanted."

"Ah. Pardon." Jamo placed another piece of soggy roll into his mouth and spoke as it dissolved. "It is something of a delicate matter."

"You wish to use my agency?"

"No, no, not at all. Not that I wouldn't. Another time, another place - "

"Another planet."

"Not that far," he smiled. "Madame Renée, it is an old matter. Something from your past."

It was her turn to smile as she put down her bowl of coffee. A small brown rim had been left on her upper lip, and Jamo wished he could lick it off. But she beat him to it with a tissue. She said softly, "Jacques."

"An easy guess, *n'est-ce pas*?"

"In some ways. He was taken from me eighteen years ago, and after the first two years things went quiet. I was left in peace. Now, it seems, the past has reawoken."

"Madame?"

"In a moment, Chief Inspector. What was your word?"

"I believe you are in danger, madame."

She said nothing and carried on eating.

He continued. "There have been killings recently. We have reason to believe they are connected to the matter Mes – Jacques – was involved in when he died. With my office, the BCP. Concerning the secret. It has raised its head again, and people are dying. One even said the name Mesrine as he died. As if Jacques had arisen from the grave seeking revenge - ridiculous, I know."

"If only."

"I believe you are in danger. You might be next on the killer's list."

"Why should I be on any killer's list, m'sieur?" she shrugged. "I have done nothing – nothing except to fall in love. I know nothing – nothing except that I know time does not heal. In my mind, Jacques is as alive today as he was eighteen years ago."

"That is the point, madame."

"What?"

"*Is* he still alive?"

She sniffed. "You are being ridiculous."

"I apologise. But someone is out there. They are searching for the secret – and they are killing."

Renée refilled their bowls and indicated the basket.

Jamo shook his head. "*Merci.*"

She looked at him, a sad, wistful look that proved – as if proof was needed – that she was still a woman in love. "I never knew what the secret was, he wouldn't tell me. Said it was for my own good. It now appears, all these years later, that my Jacques was right. There would be no reason for anyone to kill me. I do not know the secret. And I did no harm, to Jacques, to anyone."

Jamo frowned. He asked, "What are you not telling me, Sylvie?"

"What am I *not* telling you, m'sieur? Look within. Perhaps there is something I *am* telling you."

"You know who the killer is, don't you?"

"No, I do not know who it is."

"Is it you?"

"If I wanted revenge I would have taken it a long time ago. But they all died without any intervention from me."

"*Revenge?* The killer wants revenge? Not the secret? Or as well as the secret? I beg you to be open with me, Sylvie. I fear you are in great danger."

"I am in no danger."

"Tell me, please. What is it you are holding back?"

She glanced at the clock on the wall. "What I will tell you, m'sieur, is that it is now one o'clock in the morning and I am tired. I think your word is over. May I ask you to leave?"

Jamo was not pleased but he said, "Of course."

They stood up simultaneously. Sylvie's gown fell open and she made no attempt to cover herself. Neither did Jamo make any attempt not to look.

He produced his card from his pocket. "If you feel there is anything else you need to tell me, call me at any time. My mobile number is there also."

She walked him to the door. "All I wish, Chief Inspector, is to be left in peace. Despite what you think, history cannot repeat itself. Jacques is dead and," she gave a small, rueful laugh, "he has not come back to haunt us."

Jamo looked her up and down, from her head to her toes. He wondered how many men had been entertained by that magnificent body, both pre- and post- Jacques Mesrine.

"Take care, Sylvie," he said. "Madame Renée."

He turned and walked down the stairs.

Ω

Friday August 29 1997

Faubourg St Honoré, Paris, France

Claudette Ibrahim had dressed up for her 08:30 appointment at the British Embassy. Dressed up by her standards, that is. The leather biker's clothes and boots were gone, to be replaced by lightweight slingbacks, cream linen slacks and a simple white cotton T shirt. More care had been taken with her make-up.

"Claudette, hello," Ron Becker came down the grand staircase, and admired the tanned, taut arms as he shook her hand.

"It has been a while," Claudette's English was perfect. "How are you, Ronald?"

"Oh, mustn't grumble. Your new Commissioner keeping you busy?"

"Hence my visit. Your office?" She knew the way.

"Yep."

"And you. How are things?" She chatted as they climbed the stairs and made their way along the first floor corridor.

"Don't ask, my love. Don't ask. First we have a new government – always a concern, you never know what they're going to do. Cut backs in the Foreign Service and all that. And now we have this Diana business."

"Is she *ever* out of the newspapers?"

"Never. I think there was one edition of the *Daily Express* two years ago – a Monday, I think it was – when her picture did not appear. But since then she has been everywhere. Really the embassy could do without this. We get torn down the middle. We have our ambassadorial and consul duties and they do not include looking after an ex-royal who has given up official protection. On the other hand, certain parties in the UK remain concerned about her and we have to pander to their requests."

They had reached Becker's office and he closed the door behind them and motioned for Claudette to sit down. "Coffee?"

"Thank you, no."

"Do you mind if I smoke?"

"It is your office," she replied politely, shaking her head at the proffered packet. "I used to but I managed to give it up." She noted Becker's hesitation. "Please, go ahead. It does not bother me, I am past that stage now."

"You must have great willpower."

"Perhaps. When I resolve to do something, I do it."

Becker nodded admiringly as he lit up and blew a curtain of smoke between them. "So, Diana."

"Lady Di, yes."

Becker grinned at the old title by which the Princess of Wales was still known throughout the world.

"We can solve some of your problems," said Claudette.

Becker's guts moved. *If only you knew, dear French flicette with your pert little poky nips, that the solution had already been set in motion.*

"We have been asked by the Minister to provide official protection for her whenever she is in France. Our local agents will handle it when she is down on the coast. When she visits Paris, my office will handle it."

"Jesus, for God's sake don't let her know, she'll have forty fits."

"We will be discreet, of course. She will not know." *Why was the Englishman staring at her like that?* "When she is on French soil she will be under French protection. So that takes the weight off of you, *non*?"

"*Non – er, oui*. Yes. What, er, what sort of protection will you be giving her. How are you going to handle it?"

"That is what I wanted to discuss with you…"

Rue des Saussaies, Paris, France

Commissaire Gillian Colet was in a bad mood. A very bad mood. And that did not augur well for the man who now entered her office.

She waited until he had closed the door.

"And where the fuck were you last night?" she tried to repress her anger but her strained voice gave her away. "You said you were coming round."

"Gillian – " Jamo saw the frown. "*Commissaire,* excuse me. I had some urgent business. I could not get away."

"Police business, I trust?"

"Mais naturellement - "

"I would not like to think that your monthly appraisal was missed because of some private appointment." She stood up and came round the desk towards him.

"Of course not. I could not get away. I was with an informant for - "

Oh shit.

Colet stood in front of him, glasses still on the end of her nose. "Since when," she asked calmly, "does the BCP have informants?"

Oh hell.

Without warning, Colet slapped him hard across the face. "You bastard." She turned around, her back towards him.

"I am truly sorry."

"Not as sorry as you're going to be. You were with her, weren't you? Do you think I don't know the two of you have been screwing? Do you take me for an idiot?" She turned around to face him again. She had pulled her glasses off and Jamo could have sworn there was moisture in the corner of her left eye. "Do you really prefer a jumped-up little tomboy to me? A tart more suitable to the anti-riot squad than the BCP?"

"You approved her appointment last year."

"I didn't really have any choice, she applied – what the hell has that got to do with it?" She realised she was shouting. This was undignified. She stared at Jamo, breathing hard through her nose.

He said nothing. Was she going to follow-up on his informant gaff?

She gave one huge sigh, and then the vulnerable woman façade faded and the hard-faced bitch-Commissioner returned. She went back to her desk and sat down.

"Is the Inspector in?" she asked.

"No, she is visiting the British this morning. She will be Lady Di's protection when she is in Paris."

"Now that is a fitting use of her talents. I want to see her when she comes in."

"Why?"

Colet looked up. "I don't have to justify myself to *you*, Chief Inspector. If I want to talk to a member of my staff, I will do so. I do not need your permission."

"Of course not."

She started to sort through some papers on her desk.

After a moment, Jamo asked "Is that all?"

"Go." She flicked her hand at him like she was flitting away an irritating bug.

Down by his sides, Jamo's fists clenched. He turned to go.

Then, as usual, she called him back. "It really is appraisal time. As your rank no longer has staffing responsibilities, I will appraise Inspector Ibrahim this afternoon."

He did not say anything. He turned, then stopped with his back to her as she spoke again. "*Your* appraisal will take place tonight at ten o'clock. At my apartment. And this time you will keep the appointment. Do I make myself clear?"

Faubourg St Honoré, Paris, France

Inspector Claudette Ibrahim was two minutes into the five minute walk from the British Embassy to the Rue des Saussaies when her portable rang. This was the time before twee ringtone downloads, so it rang just like any other telephone.

She carried on walking down the Faubourg St Honoré as she pulled the phone from her bag.

"Allo?"

"Claudette, Pierre."

"*Oui?*"

"You still with the *rosbeefs*?"

"Just finished. I'm coming in."

"Don't. I need to talk to you, but I also need to get out of here. Before I kill someone."

"Ah now, let me guess. Couldn't be a certain Madame Commissaire, could it?"

"The fucking bitch."

"Ah, I was right then." She paused at Rue de l'Elysée until there was a break in the traffic. "Want an early lunch?"

What he really wanted was to take her back to his place and ram his frustrations out on her body, but he settled for the alternative. "Yes."

"*Henri's.* I'm almost there."

"I need a stiff one."

"That's my line, isn't it? *Deux grands calvados* and a litre of the coarsest red will await you, *mon roi.*"

Henri's Bar, Paris, France

The calvados was just a memory, as was half of the litre of red wine. Henri stood behind the bar, studying the football reports in *L'Equipe* and continuing his seventy year fight against his flatulence problem. Two old veterans of a similar vintage stood at the zinc and also participated in the farting bonding session. Old music (Claude François and Joe Dassin) came from somewhere, permeating the background.

Jamo and Ibrahim sat in a booth in a far corner. His anger was now abating, helped by a ten minute listening session by his colleague in which she had simply nodded and hmmd and hah-d, and generally agreed that Commissaire Gillian Colet was a salop of the highest order.

Claudette had an amused expression. "So let her give me my appraisal. I have no problem with that."

"She knows we're screwing."

She let the grin break across her face. "Really, how? You don't think she was watching when we stayed late that night - "

"God knows."

"She's only jealous. She probably wants to ravage you herself." Jamo said nothing. "After all, it's not often a girl comes across a true ten centimetres - "

"Hey!"

She laughed out loud. "I'll see her this afternoon."

Henri shuffled across with baguettes, cheese and two whole, raw, unpeeled onions.

With their alcohol entrées, the two police officers attacked the food with gusto. Jamo picked up an onion and bit into it like an apple, skin *et al.*

"How did things go with the British?" he asked.

"Excellent. Actually they're very pleased with us. Taken a weight off them. They cannot be seen to be protecting her now that she is no longer royal and has given up official protection. They are pleased to leave it in our hands."

"How will you do it?"

"We have also got to be discreet. But when she is on French soil she is under French jurisdiction, so we can do what we like."

"But how will you get close?"

"Well, it's not like she's under threat. The Irish won't be after her. But when she is in public she will have her own personal protection – *moi* – and she won't even know it."

She looked away teasingly and popped a piece of camembert into her mouth.

It was the first time in his life that Jamo had been jealous of a piece of cheese. "How?" he asked.

"How can I get close to Lady Di, and stay close to her, without flashing my ID? By flashing another ID!"

"What *are* you talking about?"

She rummaged in her bag and threw a plasticised card down onto the table. "It is genuine. They have a whole collection of them at the embassy. I just have to pick up a camera. Meet," she said proudly, "Mademoiselle Paparazza."

Rue des Saussaies, Paris, France

For every positive there is a negative. For every day there is a night. For every yin there is a yang.

So it was that for every good mood of Inspector Claudette Ibrahim, there was a reciprocal bad mood.

Her's occurred at 16:00 that afternoon, a cumulation of the last twenty minutes being appraised by Commissaire Gillian Colet.

Her work was good, Colet had agreed. Her investigative skills were sharp. She was worthy of her rank. But her attitude was simply not what was required in the 'diplomatic' BCP. The BCP needed negotiators, literal diplomats. Her brash, brazen attitude was more akin to the BRB or the anti riot squads.

And, announced Colet peremptorily, it was to the CRS Anti Riot Squad that Ibrahim would be transferred, straight after she had finished "this Lady Di business." Her probation in her rank was confirmed. Her probation in the BCP was over – she had failed.

And no, there was no appeal. She should expect to be moved by the end of September at the latest.

So for the second time that day, a member of staff left Colet's office with fists clenched and a desire to kill.

Jamo had gone home after the extended tactical briefing in *Henri's*. Claudette thought of going round to his place and thrusting her frustrations out on his body, but she settled for a solo return to Henri's where several more calvados and a packet of Camel awaited her. Given it up? You never give it up.

Back in her office, Commissaire Gillian Colet was pleased with herself. Both her senior members of staff sorted in one day. And Ibrahim's transfer might well stop them screwing – or if it continued at least it wouldn't be in-house.

The only in-house screwing around here was done at Commissaire level.

She wrote up the appraisal in Ibrahim's file. Nowadays, with line managers relieved of personnel duties, there was usually no need for them to see the formal report of their staff's appraisal. A verbal briefing usually sufficed. But this time she would take pleasure in letting Jamo see her full comments about his little moppet – and her dismissal from the BCP.

She would leave the file on his desk for the morning. Tonight, when he visited, she would not say a word – she hoped her mouth would be too full anyway.

Rue Vavin, Paris, France

As it was, Jamo found out about the dismissal at 17:00 – via a one-sided, foul-mouthed, 15 minute telephone tirade from Inspector Ibrahim.

He was furious, and his natural instinct was to invite Claudette around to comfort her (or at least to shag away her worries). But he could not. He had an appointment at 22:00 with The Bitch Queen, and the days were long gone when he could give both matinée and evening performances at different theatres.

So he just cluck-clucked as appropriate, promised to take the matter up tomorrow and wished Claudette well with her 'Lady Di business'.

When he put the phone down, he was pleased with himself. He thought Claudette would create when she was not invited round, but the thought seemed not to have occurred to her.

Now he had a few hours to spare, but he must remember not to shower or even wash.

For that was one of The Bitch's little secrets. The outward callous ice queen and the inward whore that was Commissaire Gillian Colet liked her men dirty.

Neuilly-sur-Seine, France

For a woman in her fifties, Gillian Colet had a reasonable body. Her breasts had grown pendulous with age, true, but the career spinster had no baby belly or stretch marks. She had two small love handles on her hips, and her thighs and upper arms were a little on the wobbly side. But all in all she was not bad.

Make-up applied, long grey hair down, washed and styled, she slipped into a diaphanous red silk kimono. Underneath she was naked save for a red silk G-string (she liked her men – her Dirty Boys, as she called them – to take it off with their mouths).

She had just put on some mood music when the doorbell rang. She looked at the clock on the escritoire: 21:45. Jamo was early. She liked it when her boys were eager.

At the salon door she gave one final look back to see that the place was tidy, and dimmed the lights to seduction level with the switch in the wall.

She undid the catch on the front door, but turned her back as the door slowly swung open. She knew he would like the view of her G-stringed bottom.

"Come in, *mon amour*," she spoke over her shoulder as she walked back to the salon. "Are you dirty?"

She heard the front door close and she could feel him coming up behind her. "Drink?" she asked.

She felt his hand touch her bottom. She smiled. He was keen. "Or do you want to just fuck?"

Now he was pushing her bottom, pushing her quickly into the salon. She almost ran with the pressure of the push, and she giggled. "My, my, you are eager. Has it been so long, Pierre? Doesn't the little tramp satisfy you?"

She wanted to throw herself down onto the settee and allow herself to be ravaged, but his hand moved from her bottom to her neck and held her tight. "Come on, Dirty Boy, do me," she encouraged, raising her head in desire.

Without warning, the kimono was ripped off her shoulders. It fell to the floor and she stood there naked save for the G-string. She closed her eyes and breathed heavily, lustfully, through her nose.

He was right up behind her now, she could feel his breath warm on her back.

A hand came round and grasped the left breast, squeezing the nipple forward in a milking motion. It hurt, but she loved it.

Then she felt the inevitable hardness pressing between the cheeks of her bottom, pressing insistently. She would not resist, she would give in willingly -

Wait a minute.

The dick was cold. It was hard and made of metal. And already it was four centimetres inside her.

"Damn fucking *salop*," said the voice in her ear.

She gasped and tried to turn, but it was too late.

Commissaire of Police Gillian Colet had no final thought. She was just aware of the fiercest and most painful and burning form of buggery she had ever experienced, and then she watched as her bowels and their contents and her womb shot out through her stomach and splattered over her settee.

She did not hear the bang of the gun. Shock killed her instantly, and the blackness of eternity had settled over her even before her legs had time to buckle.

Chief Inspector Pierre Jamo felt like a man going to his doom. Which was silly really, because it was not the first time he and Commissaire Gillian Colet had had sex. And it wasn't as if she was bad in bed – in fact she was very good, wanton and demanding, with no holes barred. But it was like the old simile: going with a promiscuous woman was like sitting on a warm lavatory seat – comfortable but you wondered who'd been there before.

As he stepped out of the small elevator, he heard a faint ringing from down the stairs. Sounded like a telephone. Then it stopped and the building was quiet.

He walked over to the glossy mahogany front door of her apartment and rang the bell. Truth be told, he was looking forward to the session with one of the wettest women he had ever been with. He smiled as his excitement stirred in his *pantalon*.

He rang the bell again. Perhaps he should get his Old Man out and have it poking at her when she opened the door? That would surprise the bitch who thought she'd seen everything. Mind you, the way he felt right now it wouldn't be pointing at her, it would be pointing at his chin! He undid his zip and pulled himself out.

He knocked on the door. Where was she? Usually she was right there waiting for him. He hoped she was wearing those G-string things. He loved the way they disappeared into the Grand Canyon of her arse. A fabric pathway into the valley of promise.

He looked at his watch. Spot on 22:00 as instructed. She would be pleased.

Now he thumped on the door. Come on baby, look what Daddy's got for you.

No reply.

This was unusual. Where was she?

And then he realised.

The bitch.

The complete fucking bitch.

She had stood him up. Because he had failed to come round last night, she had done the same to him.

The cow.

Okay honey, well it was your loss.

To prove he had been there, he popped his card through the letterbox and then turned away and walked down the stairs.

He had gone down two flights before he realised his dick was still poking out, although now just limply. Quickly he popped it back in and did up his zip.

Faubourg St Honoré, Paris, France

"Claudette? Ron Becker."

"Allo, Ron." The connection between the telephone on Becker's desk in the British Embassy and Inspector Ibrahim's portable was full of static. They could have been talking to each other from the other side of the world, not just five kilometres away.

"Sorry to call you so late," said Becker. "But we've just got news from our people that Diana will be coming to Paris tomorrow. She's in the south at the moment, on the Fayed's yacht. Her and Dodi-boy will be coming into Le Bourget in the afternoon."

"*D'accord. Merci.* Leave it with me."

Becker frowned. Usually the tough little minx from the BCP was chattier than this. Perhaps she was somewhere she couldn't talk. "Do you have everything you need?"

"Yes, thank you. I will be around her."

"Okay. And thanks once again for taking this off our hands." But the static had won its battle and they could not hear each other.

Montmartre, Paris, France

Unusually for a cat, Will liked having her ears touched. She sat in the woman's arms and let her ears be stroked upwards, at the same time twitching them as she stared at a pigeon on the roof tiles outside the window.

The woman absentmindedly stroked the cat's ears and thought of other things.

It had never been her intention to kill Madame Renée – Sylvie Jacquot. Why should she? Unlike the others, Sylvie had not been instrumental in her father's death, she had not influenced events. She was just a pawn, a woman who had fallen in love.

And yet her information had been the most helpful of all.

So now events would need to go in the other direction – the British. She had seen to the French, now the final vengeance was drawing near. She knew there was a man at the embassy who had been there eighteen years ago. Was he involved in her father's death? Either directly or indirectly? And did he know the secret? She now knew without doubt that the answer to both questions was yes.

Her father had discovered the British secret. His involvement with it had led directly to his death. Now she would find out what her father had known. It was Daddy's legacy.

And in return she would give him British blood.

Boulevard Exelmans, Paris, France

Ron Becker and Gisele Joudeh, the Lebanese diplomat, were lying side by side in bed. Gisele was asleep and Ron looked at her admiringly, enjoying the regal countenance and thinking warm – and naughty – thoughts about what they had been doing just half an hour before.

Ron could not sleep – unusual for a man who had just made love. It was the first time Gisele had failed to knock him out with her carnal skills. Ron was thinking of another woman, and not in a sexual sense (although many men had): Diana, Princess of Wales.

Were they really going to kill her?

He laughed inwardly. Of course they bloody well were, he had set it in motion, hadn't he? And once the Russian was on a tail, it was hard to call him off. The one fax number was the only way to contact him. If he had already gone off on the hunt, he was unreachable.

Becker had been responsible for many deaths before, it was part of his job. Particularly he remembered the carnage back in 1979. How many people had died all together? Personally he had pulled the trigger on Robert Lensens and his wife, had had Paul Richer in his sights (before Mesrine had unwittingly done the job for him), and had planted and primed the device that killed Chief Inspector Claude Gerard.

That had been the biggest and most concentrated glut of killings in his career. In fact, Gerard had been the last person he had actually murdered himself. Since then, he had either ordered, blackmailed or paid others to do it. There hadn't been that many (nowhere near three figures), but Wallis Simpson in 1986 had been the most high profile.

Until now.

This time it was almost regicide – or was it not regicide if one royal killed another? Was the old woman back in England really going to do it? Clearly, yes. And why was obvious. It could only be one thing: the damned secret. Somehow Diana had found out. And like the rest before her, she was to die.

His musings were interrupted by his mobile phone flashing on the bedside table. It was on silent, but it gave off a gentle vibration.

He pulled himself up and sat on the edge of the bed, reaching for the phone. Gisele still slept soundly.

He did not recognise the number and he carried the throbbing instrument out of the bedroom before pressing the green button.

"Hello, Ron Becker," he answered lowly as he walked into the *salle de jour*.

"Monsieur Becker? I am sorry to call you at such a late hour." The voice was female, accented. "This is Commissaire Gillian Colet of the BCP. We haven't actually met."

"Ah, Commissaire, good evening. A pleasure to talk to you. Even at midnight. What can I do for you?"

"It is about Lady Diana - "

"The Princess, yes."

"I wonder if I could come round to see you? I know it is late but something urgent has arisen. We believe there may be a threat to Lady Di while she is here."

Shit. Did the frogs know something? They couldn't. Impossible.

"Well, er, of course. I'm not at the embassy, I'm at home."

"I know. I am outside in my car, now. Can I come up?"

His eyebrows rose. "You are outside?"

"Forgive my temerity. It is very urgent I see you."

"All right, come on up. Ring the bell – the top one – and I'll buzz you in."

Becker waited for the knock on the door. He had never met Commissaire Gillian Colet, but he had heard a lot about her from Jamo and Ibrahim. Apparently she was a bitch and then some.

What *had* she got wind of? Couldn't be anything to do with HM's instructions. Only Her Majesty, Sir Kenneth Dean, himself and, of course, the contractor knew what was to happen. There could not have been a leak. It must be something else. Was someone else after Diana?

The knock on the door was firm but low, like the secret knock of a lover asking to be let in.

Becker opened the door, knowing it was not a lover.

But neither was it Commissaire Gillian Colet.

The woman was dressed in black leather. Becker's mouth dropped open. At first he could not understand. *"Claudette?"*

The body was that of Claudette Ibrahim, but the look in the eyes revealed someone else's soul within. She held a gun in both hands, and it was pointing straight at Becker's head. "Get inside."

"Claudette?"

"Inside."

Becker stumbled backwards as she came in and kicked the door closed behind her. "What the fuck is this?" he demanded.

"Are you alone?"

"Y – yes."

"The kitchen. Where is it?"

"Over there."

"Lead me."

"Now just a minute, I think you've got some explaining to - "

The gun touched against the exact centre of his forehead. Her nose was flared. "I have no explaining to do, Englishman. In the kitchen. Now."

Becker turned and led the way to the second door along the dim corridor. There were only a few lights on. He kept his arms by his side.

She flicked the switch for the overhead fluorescent. "Sit down at the table," she ordered. "Put your hands on the top, palms upwards."

"I don't understand - "

"Just do it. There is nothing you need to understand." She looked around the small kitchen as Becker sat down. Her eyes stopped on a liquidiser next to the microwave. She smiled and then shook her head. Reaching over, she took a large carving knife from a block and examined the end for sharpness.

"Inspector Ibrahim," said Becker. "I - "

"Do not use that name. That is somebody else."

Becker frowned then shook his head in bewilderment. He was completely confused.

She pulled out a chair, right-angled it to Becker, turned it around and straddled it. The gun remained pointed at the Englishman. "Now," she twirled the carving knife around in her left hand. "Tell me what you know."

In the bedroom at the far end of the corridor, Gisele Joudeh reluctantly allowed herself to wake up from a delicious post-coital sleep. She did not want to come round just yet, but her bladder was insistent.

She stretched and felt the empty place in the bed next to her. It took a moment to register. Then she wondered. Where was Ronald?

Becker was puzzled. How the hell did the French know about the hit on Diana? Had there been a lapse? Security was usually so tight. When the British wanted to kill, 'need to know' was enforced with a strictness unrivalled in any other area. A maximum of four: the Instigator, the Catalyst, the Rag, the Contractor. Sometimes Becker was the Contractor; usually, as in this case, he was the Rag. Third in line: the Queen Mother, Sir Kenneth Dean, himself, Ramirov.

"How did you find out?" he asked.

"That is your last question," said the woman who did not want to be called Ibrahim. "Do not ask anything more. Tell me what you know."

Ω

Sleepily, Gisele pulled herself up into a sitting position on the side of the bed. She could hear muffled voices. Did Ronald have the TV on? At this hour? Surely he wasn't watching filth again?

She stood up and stretched.

"I am but an oily rag," explained Becker. "You must understand that. I do what I am told. When my masters say 'Jump', I say 'How high?'. I don't ask questions. I do what I am told." He paused. The woman sitting opposite him, legs straddled over the chair, gun in one hand, knife in the other, stared at him silently.

"The order came through two weeks ago. Look, it probably won't happen in Paris, so you've no need to worry. You won't be compromised or implicated."

Still she said nothing.

He shrugged. "They have ordered Diana killed, what can I say?"

Claudette showed no reaction. Her face was stone.

"I don't ask why – that's how I've survived," continued Becker. "My God, the things I know! Look, Claudette, are you - erm - are you sure this is diplomatically correct - ?"

The movement of the knife was just a blur.

Gisele padded naked down the corridor. She would have her pee and then she would give Ronald hell for even thinking of watching porn after what she had done to him earlier – she could still feel his stubble burn on her inner thighs.

She was one metre away from the kitchen door when she heard the scream.

The knife sliced through the palm of Ron Becker's upturned left hand, pinning it to the wooden table. There was one squirt of blood that rose thirty centimetres into the air.

"Fucking hell!" he screamed.

Claudette grabbed his left wrist with her gun hand. "Be still," she instructed softly, calmly, almost sensually. "Your natural reaction is to jerk your hand. Do not. You will cause more damage."

"What the fuck - "

"I told you no more questions. You did not obey me."

"I..."

"Eighteen years ago," said Claudette gently. "You were responsible for the death of my father."

"*What?*"

"The Mesrine affair."

Becker opened his mouth, stunned.

"Your *father?*"

"He was killed because he knew your British secret."

"And you have come to avenge him, I suppose. How the hell did you become a policeman?"

She gave a little flick with her finger on the top of the knife.

Becker's whole body stiffened as pain shot up through his wrist. "*Shit!*"

"I want to know what the secret is."

"You're crazy," said Becker, and he winced in preparation for another flick. It did not come. "Anyone who knows the secret, dies. That's the point, don't you see? *I* don't know it. I just have to arrange the deaths of everyone who does. If I knew it, *I* would be killed."

"Who knows it? Someone must. Who is ordering the deaths?"

"England."

"What do you mean 'England'?"

"Her Majesty?"

"Your Queen?"

"No, she does not know. It's her mother."

"And she is the only one who knows?"

"Her and Di - " Becker stopped as he suddenly realised he might have made a big mistake. A very big mistake. The French did *not* know about the hit on Diana. And now he had told them.

"Diana?" said Claudette. "Lady Di? She knows?" She let it sink in. "Oh my God, and that's why you are going to kill her?"

"It has been ordered."

"You crazy bastards."

"I do as I am told."

"Only obeying orders, huh? Where have I heard that before?"

Becker was looking around, trying to find a way out, a way to stop this. "Look, your father, he was a criminal."

Her face turned nasty. "He was not! My father was never a criminal. He was a good man," she snarled into his face. "He - "

At that moment, a naked woman appeared in the kitchen doorway and fired at Claudette from two metres.

Rue Vavin, Paris, France

Pierre Jamo drove his Fiat Uno down Rue Vavin and parked as near as he could to his apartment block. The small southern part of the road was quiet at midnight, but down on the main Boulevard, Montparnasse was still humming.

He was still obsessing over that damn bitch Colet as he let himself into the building, walked past the shuttered concierge's lodge and pressed the button for the lift.

He wondered if he should call Claudette? Perhaps it wasn't too late to salvage the evening. She might still come over, if he asked nicely. Or perhaps she would invite him over to her place in Montmartre? He had yet to be granted the honour of screwing her in her own bed.

He felt for his portable, and then thought better of it. He would use the landline indoors.

He let himself into his flat quietly, so as not to disturb his fellow residents in the block. Throwing his jacket across the back of an armchair, he picked up the telephone. He knew her numbers by heart, both home and mobile. He keyed the seven-digit home number.

After ten rings he gave up. Either she was not at home or she was not answering. Perhaps she was asleep? Or perhaps she was entertaining someone? They had never agreed that their relationship was exclusive.

He stood with the phone in his hand, wondering if he should call her portable?

What the hell, he had nothing to lose.

He dialled the eleven-digit code.

Boulevard Exelmans, Paris, France

It all happened at once.

In real time it took just three seconds, but for the participants it played out in slow-motion.

Claudette was snarling into Becker's face when she was aware of the shadow in the doorway. As she turned to look, she saw the flash from Gisele's gun. She felt the heat as the bullet missed her cheek by one centimetre, and then felt hot wetness hit her as the bullet tore into Becker's head, blowing away the left side of his brain.

Claudette turned her gun and fired instinctively at the naked woman. At the same time she pushed herself backwards off the chair.

The bullet hit Gisele in the neck, and blood spurted across the kitchen wall as the Lebanese was thrown fully across the hallway, crashing into the wall and falling limply.

Claudette lay on her back, slightly winded. Then she raised herself up onto her elbows and looked from one body to the other. Becker was laying back in the chair, eyes and mouth open. Some of his brain was stuck to the wall. She spat as she realised some of his brain was stuck to her face also.

The naked woman – *who the hell was she?* – lay twisted in the hallway like a shattered rag doll. Blood rolled slowly from her neck, across her chest and down between the cavity of her breasts. A little further down, the body was pissing itself.

It was then that Claudette's portable phone began to ring.

Ω

Saturday August 30 1997

Paris, France

10:00 Rue des Saussaies

Chief Inspector Pierre Jamo strolled into the office. He was working Saturdays that week, and should have been in by 08:00 at the latest. But he didn't really care. He was pissed off. Blown out twice in one night. Once by the Bitch Colet and then by Claudette who had not been answering her phones. And now here in the office there was no one else around.

Claudette would be out on Diana patrol (and racking up some good overtime in the process), and the whore Colet never worked weekends if she could help it (what Commissaire did?). No doubt The Bitch would be expecting him to contact her and ask her where she had been last night, but he would not do that. He was not going to play her little game. When he saw her on Monday, he would pretend nothing had happened.

He entered the office carrying his staple breakfast of a packet of *Gauloises*, one croissant in a grease-proof bag and an espresso – all from *Henri's*. This morning it was a double espresso. Perhaps, he thought, he should have ordered a triple. He had had such a bad night, in fact he had hardly slept at all.

His disgruntlement with the two women aside, something else had been nagging at him. During his intermittent bouts of sleep, he had dreamt of two huge, disembodied tits wearing a peroxide wig. They had been speaking to him, trying to tell him something. During his frequent bouts of nocturnal consciousness, he had thought of Sylvie Jacquot, Mesrine's wife-that-was-not-to-be.

Something she had said…

He noticed a blue folder on his desk. He read the cover as he sat down and tore open his croissant bag. Ibrahim, **Claudette Maria**. It was her personnel file. He had not seen it before. There had been no need to, now that staffing functions on Inspectors and above were all handled at Commissaire level. Why was the folder here now?

He grunted. The Bitch Colet had put it there, of course. On the top would be Claudette's appraisal report of yesterday and – to rub salt into his wound – her dismissal from the BCP and transfer to the CRS Anti Riot Squad.

Jamo popped the last piece of croissant into his mouth. He opened the folder. He would not read The Bitch Colet's report, but he would sneak a little look at *l'histoire* of the woman who had been his fuck-mate for the last few months. It would be nice to know something about her.

He picked up his espresso.

It took one minute and fifty-three seconds for it all to fall into place. For it to hit home. For everything to become clear.

It hit him like an RER express train ramming into his testicles and disappearing out his arse.

The paper coffee cup shot across his desk, espresso decorating the folder in front of him.

Oh, Holy God.

Now he remembered what Sylvie Jacquot had said. Now he *understood* what Sylvie Jacquot had said.

"What am I not telling you, m'sieur? Look within. Perhaps there is something I *am* telling you."

Look within. *Look within.*

He stared at the file in front of him, now stained with a miasma of brown. Something *he* had said came back to him also. He had said that the killings were not directly linked to Mesrine, that the supercriminal was secondary, a bit-player.

How right he had been. Only until now he had not known why.

He read the page in front of him again.

Claudette Ibrahim. Married for a few months in her early twenties to one Joseph Ibrahim. A marriage that did not last, but she had kept her husband's surname. But before that she had been known by her birth name.

For Claudette Ibrahim had been born Claudette Gerard.

She was the daughter of Chief Inspector Claude Gerard, late of the BCP.

The third victim of The Mesrine Conclusion.

The man who had been blown up in the Rue Lamarck.

Eighteen years ago.

Because he knew the secret.

PART FOUR

Ω

CULMINATION

Jamo snatched up the telephone on his desk and thumped out Claudette's home number. After ten rings he pressed the bridge of the phone and then keyed her portable.

It just rang and rang. No response. She had probably turned it off.

Jamo hoped he was wrong about this. Surely Claudette was not a serial killer?

This was perverse. Had he actually ordered Claudette to investigate murders she had committed? Had he sent her chasing *herself*?

He sat back in his chair and puffed out his cheeks. He had been played. Well and truly played.

She had joined the BCP twelve months ago, a tenacious, pugnacious little Inspector promoted from the *Police Judiciare*. The BCP had been her choice. Naturally in her new post she had access to all the diplomatically sensitive files. Files going back to the inception of the BCP in 1974. All files. Files that would contain names. Including the names of all those involved in the Mesrine affair in 1979.

Literally the murders had been an inside job! She was out for revenge. And she was out for something else too: the secret. The reason they all had died then, the reason she was killing them all now.

Again Jamo picked up the telephone. He needed guidance. He keyed The Bitch Colet's home number. She would be pissed at being disturbed on a Saturday, but it would serve her right, payback for standing him up last night.

The phone rang. And rang.

No answer.

She could be away for the weekend, reasoned Jamo.

He put the phone down. He looked up a number in his desk diary and once more grabbed the receiver.

This time he got an answer. "British Embassy."

"Good morning, Mr Ron Becker please. This is Chief

Inspector Jamo of the BCP."

"One moment, please."

Becker's extension rang. And rang. No response.

This time Jamo lost it. Damn and blast. Would nobody speak to him? He banged the receiver up and down on his desk in rage. The top of the phone flew off towards Claudette's desk.

Fucking hell.

He grasped the edge of his desk and fought to control his temper.

Slowly his furious breathing subsided to normal.

He fumbled in his jacket pocket for his packet of Gauloises. Nowadays this was a non-smoking building but, quite frankly, he didn't give a shit.

Right, he thought. Time to do things on his own.

10:35 Gare du Nord

The 06:25 *Eurostar* from London Waterloo arrived just a few minutes late (a track problem – 'refugees' – at Calais-Frethun).

John Smith, Head of 'Charles' People', smiled farewell to the neatly-uniformed hostess standing by the door and disembarked from the First Class coach.

He walked along the platform with his fellow travellers and was swallowed up by the throng on the concourse of the station.

Outside, he waited in line for a cab…

11:00 Montmartre

Time was, the streets of Paris would be empty in August. Over two-thirds of the city would be shut down for the month for the *'Fermeture Annuelle'*. But this annual *en bloc* taking of holidays had dwindled over the years, so that by the end of the second millennium it was respected only by the old folk, an anachronistic reminiscence, harking back to the good old days when there was order, structure, and it was good to be alive. Nowadays life was simply chaos and disorder.

So the streets of Montmartre were teeming with traffic, despite it being August. Saturday meant that there weren't so many lorries and delivery vans on the capital's crowded streets, but this was more than compensated by the hoards of tourists, wandering into the roads without thought, brains left at Immigration.

Jamo took the back way, going around the western side of the *butte* via Place Clichy and Rue Caulaincourt. He had found Claudette's address on file: 1 Rue Lamarck.

It took him two double-backs to find a parking space, and eventually he settled for the tightest of spots outside the Hotel Roma. From there it was a five minute walk.

The top bell button said Ibrahim C. He put his finger on it and left it there. Somewhere up above it must be ringing.

But there was no reply, no voice over the entry phone.

He pushed the bottom button marked Concierge and waited.

Shortly the door was opened by a cropped-haired scruffy young man, a student type. *"M'sieur?"*

Jamo flashed his ID. "Police. I wish to see Madame Ibrahim, I'm getting no reply."

"I think Claudy's away for the weekend - "

Jamo pushed past him. *Claudy?* "I'll find out for myself."

The concierge shrugged as Jamo began his trot up the stairs.

11:05 Gare du Nord

Half an hour to wait for a cab. Well, thought John Smith, glad to see that some things are the same in Paris as they are in London.

His turn came and he climbed into the old Renault. The driver was a woman in her sixties, grey hair dyed yellow, with matching teeth and slightly darker nicotine-stained fingers. Next to her sat an equally yellow-tinged white poodle, who took one look at Smith and decided it had something better to do – sleep.

"*L'ambassade de Grande Bretagne,*" said Smith.

11:10 Montmartre

After two flights, Jamo wished there was a lift in this old building. After five flights, he thought of paying for one himself. After six flights, he wished he was dead.

He stood outside Claudette's door, bending forward, regaining control of his breathing. He reached for his *Gauloises*, took one out of the packet, stared at it and then put it back.

He rapped on the door. "Claudette?"

He could hear nothing from inside. "Claudette? It's me, Pierre."

This time he heard something. Sounded like a drawer or a door being closed. He rapped again. "Claudette! Open up!"

There were no footsteps inside, no sound of locks being unlocked or bolts being unbolted.

Okay, the last time she had to do this for him. This time he was on his own.

He stood back, lifted his right leg, achieved his balance and kicked mightily at the door.

It took three kicks, and then the door shot backwards, the old wood splintering around the lock.

"Claudette?" He had his gun in his hand as he eased his way along the hallway. The three doors were closed. "It's Pierre. Come out please."

He tried the door on his left. The bathroom. Empty.

Then he tried the one on his right. A bedroom. Bed unmade. An old stuffed Snoopy between the pillows. From the doorway his eyes moved over her dressing table: various perfumes and girlie things adorned the top. He gave an ironic grunt at the open box of Tampax.

Then he heard a sound again. Coming from the next room. Gun raised and pointing at the ceiling, he turned the door handle. Then he stood back as his push made the door creak slowly open.

"Claudette?" He peeked into the salon and then relaxed. "No, you are not Claudette." He put the gun down by his side as he came in. "You must be Will, I've heard a lot about you."

The cat looked up at him from the settee and mewed. Then, as if she had suddenly remembered that she needed to, she began to lick her left paw with intensity.

"Where is she pussycat, huh?" Jamo came over and sat next to the animal. He stroked the soft red-tabby fur. "Where has she gone?"

His eyes were caught by a manila folder sitting on the coffee table in front of him. Cautiously he reached forward and flicked it open. Then he frowned and leant forward some more, fanning all the sheets out over the glass.

There they all were. Charles Fleury-Goujon, Veronique Lensens, Sylvie Jacquot. Photographs, biographies and, importantly, hand written comments. Comments on their links with the Mesrine affair nearly twenty years ago.

Jamo noticed there was something underneath the picture of Sylvie Jacquot. He moved the picture to find another one below. It made his jaw drop.

It was slightly blurred and had been taken without the subject knowing. The person was younger in the picture than he was now, but without doubt it was him.

Ron Becker of the British Embassy.

"Weow!" said the cat.

11:30 Faubourg St Honoré

John Smith paid off the cab and walked through the large black doors of the British Embassy and into the ornate lobby.

A plain-clothes security guard was on duty, but in 1997 one could walk, observed but unhindered, over to the Reception desk.

"Good morning, sir," the middle aged receptionist spoke in French. "Can I help you?"

"I'm here to see Mr Becker," said Smith, noticing how the receptionist's aura relaxed infinitesimally as she heard him speak English. "Mr Ron Becker. I'm from Special Branch, UK." He showed his ID.

The receptionist looked at it, but she knew better than to try to touch it.

"Mr Becker has not come in this morning, Mr – er – Smith. We don't know quite where he is. Would you care to wait or leave a message?"

It crossed Smith's mind to ask for the ambassador, Sir Michael Jay, but then he thought better of it. What he had to do was not for the ambassador's 'need to know'.

"You've no idea when Mr Becker will be in?"

"No, Mr Smith. Or indeed if he will be."

"Okay. I'll leave my number. Please ask him to ring me as soon as he turns up." He took a card from his pocket. "I can be contacted there."

"I'll see that he gets this as soon as he comes in. Will he know what it's about?"

"If he doesn't, he'll find out soon enough."

Smith turned and walked back across the tiled marble floor. He reached the front door and stood aside to let a man enter, a medium-height, paunchy, black haired man who, from his rosy cheeks, looked like he was in something of a hurry.

Smith went out.

The man hurried over to the reception desk, with the security guard looking at him intently.

"Good morning, sir," the middle aged receptionist spoke in French. "Can I help you?"

"I'm here to see Mr Becker," said the man. "Chief Inspector Pierre Jamo of the BCP."

11:40 Eastwards

John Smith decided to walk to his next destination. It was a fine Parisian summer's day and it would only take fifteen minutes.

He headed east along Rue du Faubourg St Honoré for the straight-line walk to Rue de Castiglione.

11:45 Henri's Bar

Pierre Jamo decided to walk to his next destination also. His walk would take just five minutes.

He headed west along Rue du Faubourg St Honoré and then cut up Rue de Duras. He soon found himself entering Henri's Bar.

Jamo was never one to succumb to the mawkishness caused by alcohol, but he was susceptible to anger – with or without booze. He was angry now. Where the fuck was everybody? Colet, Claudette, Becker. All missing.

"Two calvados and two glasses of paint stripper," he said to Henri, who grunted and began to place glasses on the *zinc*, shot glasses for the calvados not brandy bowls because he knew the policeman liked it that way.

"Tell me something, *Henri mon ami*," Jamo watched the calvados being poured. "What do you do when no one wants to speak to you?"

The old bar owner sniffed. "Doesn't happen in my job, m'sieur. Everyone talks to me. I am their counsellor, their psychiatrist. They all confide in old Henri. I could tell you some things, m'sieur! Even the men from your Department – "

Something occurred to Jamo. "How far back do you remember?"

"I have seventy years, m'sieur – and I remember every one of them!"

Jamo knocked back the first calvados in one. "A man called Claude Gerard, a Chief Inspector. Nearly twenty years ago. Remember him?" The second calvados disappeared like the first, and Jamo belched loudly.

"Claude Gerard..." Henri was looking at a point way behind Jamo. Eighteen years behind. "Oh, yes. He died, didn't he? Blown up in his car. It was the time of *Le Grand*, the great Jacques."

"What was he like? Gerard."

Henri's eyes came back to rest on Jamo. "What can I say, m'sieur? He was a regular customer. He was... How can I say this? A slob, a nasty piece of work. Excuse me, m'sieur." Henri went off to serve some new arrivals.

Jamo started on his red wine. *A nasty piece of work.* Did that mean he was a murdering piece of work? And had the murdering genes passed to his daughter?

He felt a trembling next to his right testicle.

For a second he thought it was the booze. Then he realised his portable was in his pocket. He took it out, still vibrating and ringing. He couldn't see who it was in the dim light of the bar – and he certainly wouldn't be able to hear with Dalida singing her stuff through the speakers.

Signalling to Henri to leave his wine where it was, he went outside, squinting as the sun hit him. He answered the phone.

"Where the fuck is my cat?" said a raised female voice.

11:55 Rue Cambacérès

"Claudette?"

"It was you, wasn't it? In my apartment. Did you have to kick the fucking door in? Will got out."

"I'm sorry, I – Where the hell are you? I've been trying to contact you."

"I've had things to do. Still have."

"I know, Claudette. I know about your father."

"That bitch left you my file, right?"

"Has it been you? The killings?"

"I just want to know why they killed him. I must know the British secret."

"Come in. Stop this nonsense."

"Nonsense! So my father is nonsense, is he?"

"I didn't mean - "

"I have a job to do and I will see it through. Did you know I'm being transferred to the CRS? Of course you do, I told you. Colet's last act as Commissioner."

"What do you mean, her last - " Oh God.

"There's a vacancy, *Pierre mon amour*. Could be yours."

Claudette was mad. Quite mad.

"But I tell you one thing," she continued. "If my cat does not come back, I'm going to put a skewer through your scrotum and kebab your balls while you're still alive."

She hung up.

12:00 Place Vendôme

John Smith entered The Ritz Hotel by its main doors on the Place Vendôme. His smart-casual fawn cotton trousers and blue open-necked shirt did not look out of place in the 4-star Fayed establishment *[there is no official 5-star designation for hotels in France]*, but his battered, lived-in face looked like it would be more at home in the back streets of Pigalle.

He went over to the Concierge desk. A smartly-uniformed grey-haired gentleman greeted him. *"Oui, monsieur?"*

"Bonjour. The Director of Security, *s'il vous plait."*

There was just a momentary pause before the concierge asked, "Who shall I say is calling, sir?"

"A friend of Mr Jones. The Director knows him."

"Un ami de Monsieur Jones. D'accord." There was just a hint of reluctance – or perhaps suspicion. Then the concierge picked up a remarkably old – or *faux* old – telephone and keyed an internal number. He had a discussion with someone in rapid French, then he put the phone down.

"Je regrette, the Director is out, monsieur. His assistant will see you momentarily."

Smith nodded his thanks and moved away from the desk to let an American couple berate the concierge about the quantity of towels in their room (they were quickly referred to Housekeeping).

Smith looked around the elegant lobby, and was impressed. *You've done a great job in restoring this to its former glory, Mohamed.*

He waited.

"Monsieur, you were asking for the Director?"

Smith turned. He was expecting someone in uniform. What he saw was a fortysomething matronly woman, dressed in a blouse and trousers with just the right amount of class and elegance to make her fit into her surroundings perfectly. Of course, Smith thought, the Ritz Security Team would need to blend, not to publicise their presence.

"Yes," he said. "I believe he's out."

"At the moment, but we are expecting him back later. May I help you?"

"I'm just a friend of a friend. I was in Paris, and my friend suggested I pop in and say hello. Nothing important. But I go home tomorrow, so I thought if he was free later perhaps we could get together."

"Are you staying at the hotel, *m'sieur?*"

"Regrettably no. But if I give you my telephone number, could you ask him to call me?"

"Your phone works in France, *m'sieur?*"

"Yes, no problem." It works in places you couldn't begin to imagine, lady. He produced a card from his shirt pocket. It contained simply his name and mobile phone number.

She took it and read it. Then she said, *"D'accord, Monsieur... Smith.* I will see that Monsieur Henri Paul gets this."

12:15 Rue des Saussaies

Chief Inspector Pierre Jamo hurried through the Cambacérès entrance and took the nearest elevator up to the sixth floor. He walked through the labyrinthine connecting corridors until he came out in the building that was 11 Rue des Saussaies.

He heard the scraping of a chair from the General Office as he passed by, and Sergeant Maurice Goise caught up with him as Jamo was opening the door to the Inspectors' Office.

"Chief, Chief!"

Jamo continued on in with Goise behind him. *"Oui?"* He stood in front of Claudette's desk, staring at it, as if wondering what to do.

"They say they've left messages on your ansaphone, but they came though to me also. Apparently it's extremely urgent, although I can't recall them bothering us before."

"Jesus, Maurice," Jamo looked up. "Can't somebody else take it? I'm very busy. Give it to Inspector - " He looked at the empty desk.

"They were asking for you specifically, Chief. I asked them to leave me details but they wouldn't. They just asked that you contact them urgently. As if it was yesterday."

"If it was that urgent why didn't you phone me?"

Goise smiled and relaxed his shoulders. "You told me you were going to Henri's after the embassy. Nothing is so urgent to disturb a man's quiet time."

Jamo smiled also. "So what is it?"

"The Lebanese Embassy, Chief. They're asking that you call them right away."

13:00 Saint Denis

Saint Denis on the northern borders of Paris could at that time best be described as working class. True, the impressive Stade de France had given the area a much-needed boost in self-esteem, but it could not hide the fact that this area consisted predominantly of factories and social housing.

It was on the Rue des Poissoniers, outside a graffiti-daubed block, bed linen hanging out of the open windows of the apartments above, that the bald-headed man found what he was looking for.

People who live in social housing (the projects, council houses, call them what you will) soon learn the basics of security. You keep your doors locked at all times. Your windows, if you are on the lower floors, you keep locked at all times also, even if you are in. You only leave outside what must be left outside. If possible, cars and bikes should be kept in lock-ups.

The rider of this motorbike had a lock-up, and he was going there shortly. But first he had to leave his heavy parcel, which he had balanced perilously on his fuel tank all the way from Porte de la Villette, outside his front door on the ground floor. Leaving his engine running, he dismounted and bumped the parcel through the main doors to the building and over to his apartment just in on the right.

Just ten seconds after he had gone through the main doors, he came back out.

And his bike was gone.

13:45 Neuilly-sur-Seine

Jamo stood outside the door of the apartment of Commissaire Gillian Colet, as he had done sixteen hours previously. Only this time he didn't have his dick hanging out.

This time he had come prepared. He held a crowbar in his left hand, his Glock 17 in his right.

One knock on the door. No answer of course. She would never answer a door again.

The wood splintered, and he kicked the door open. The smell hit him immediately, and he gagged.

He tucked the crowbar under his arm, covered his nose and mouth with his hand, and quickly but cautiously went over to the salon door.

"Gillian?" His voice was muffled behind his hand. He pushed the door open with his foot, pointed the gun out in front of him, and went inside.

The sight was astonishing and disgusting. She had been blown almost in half. She was naked and she was kneeling on the floor in front of the settee. Her top half was on the chair, and it was connected to her legs only by a squashed mess of various glistening red entrails and gleaming white bone. It was as if she was expecting to take a lover doggy-style.

It was that final thought that did it. Jamo felt it coming and there was nothing he could do about it. With an inhuman roar he vomited with alarming ferocity over the body. Not once, not twice, but three times.

A total and utter waste of good calvados and Henri's *vin rouge* paint stripper.

14:45 Place de Clichy

The European Union is intended to be one big country – that is why the countries that belong to the Union are called Member *States*. One of the concepts of this mega-country is that once a person has crossed the frontier and immigration controls of one 'State' he or she is free to travel at will throughout the rest of the States – akin to travelling between one county and another in England, or one region to another in Italy, one state to another in the US.

Whilst to a degree this happens, the Member States of the EU still retain a normal record of 'foreigners' on their soil, usually by hotel checks. Visiting foreigners are required to hand over their passport at Reception, either for it to be retained for 24 hours or for a copy of the details page to be taken there and then.

A way round this is to be a native. Home nationals are required to present nothing at check-in, save perhaps for a credit card imprint.

So it was that French national Ito Rennes checked into the 3-star Hotel Mercure Montmartre just north of the Place de Clichy that afternoon. He was a pleasant man with a pronounced Normandy accent. His completely bald head was pink, and he made a point of explaining to the clerk that he was on his way home from his *vacances* motor-biking on the south coast and had decided to stop off in Paris on his way back.

How long would he be staying?

Just the one night.

Up in his room, Ito Rennes peeled of his biker's leathers and stepped into the shower. It felt strange to be in Paris where Ilych Ramirez Sanchez was supposedly awaiting trial for his crimes, just a few kilometres to the south, over the river, in La Santé Prison. He hoped the stool-pigeon enjoyed his lifetime in a

French jail. At least the poor schmuck knew that his family in Venezuela were well taken care of - pity the prisoner had never thought to ask the definition of 'taken care of'!

Rennes laughed as he let the water cascade over his bald head and over his body. But, he thought, he would get the job done – here, today – and then be off. Two murders of royalty in one place was enough. Wallis Simpson eleven years ago and now Diana today. History was, literally, repeating itself!

He stretched out and slowly turned the shower knob to its maximum heat. The water became uncomfortable, but it was by no means scalding.

Then something strange began to happen. The bald head started to peel away under the hot water, as if he was being burned or had suddenly been afflicted by instant leprosy. Then the mat of hair on his chest began to fall bit by bit into the shower tray, with flesh attached.

Ito Rennes ran his hands over his scalp and pulled the skin away from his head…

Twenty minutes later, Ian Ramsey stood in front of the mirror. Looking back at him was another person. The man had cropped black hair, greying at the temples; his chest was hairless and he was several kilos lighter than Ito Rennes.

Ramsey smiled, felt in his toiletries bag and brought out what looked like a fifteen centimetre long black caterpillar. Using the tiniest tube of prosthetic glue, he stuck it on his upper lip, flexed it a few times and was content.

He went back to his toiletries bag and brought out his wide tin of shaving soap which had accompanied him all the way from the USA. He prised off the lid, then took the tin in his hands and unscrewed the top containing the two millimetre layer of soap.

He was left with a round metal object twenty-five centimetres in diameter.

Right, time to get rid of this little bitch 'naturally'. Then he could go home. He looked at his watch lying on the bedside table. She would be arriving about now.

15:15 Le Bourget

Le Bourget airfield is seven kilometres to the north of Paris. The Fayed jet touched down smoothly after its one hour flight from Olbia, Sardinia. On board were Diana, Dodi Fayed, their bodyguards, a few assistants and crew.

Meeting the plane were two vehicles from The Ritz Hotel: a Mercedes 600 and a back-up Range Rover. There were just a handful of photographers.

Diana, Dodi and his bodyguard would travel in the Mercedes. Henri Paul and Les Wingfield would travel in the Range Rover, together with the luggage.

By 15:30 disembarkation was complete, and the vehicles set off on their journey into Paris. Their first destination was a house now owned by Mohamed Al Fayed on a 50 year lease from the Mayor of Paris. It was a house where Dodi hoped to set up home with his future wife. It was in western Paris. Number 24, Boulevard Suchet, at one time the residence of the Duke and Duchess of Windsor...

On the edge of the airfield, a leather-clad figure in a red crash helmet watched the cars drive away. Then she climbed back onto her Ducati M900 and followed at a safe distance.

15:30 Rue de Berri

In their room in the Hotel California in Rue de Berri just off the Champs Elysées, Christina Cascianis and Melanie Nathanson looked at the laptop screen.

Over a secure link from Tel Aviv via Rome, Barking Dog was accessing the Interior Ministry server to discover all foreign nationals who had checked into Paris hotels in the previous forty-eight hours.

"If he does not use a hotel, we are sunk," said Christina.

"Oh he will, hun, he will," reassured Melanie. "You can bet on it. Hotels are impersonal places, especially the big ones. People come, people go. He wants to just slip in and out – as they say."

But Christina was uncertain. "What if he hass a private apartment or iss staying with someone?"

Melanie touched the Greek woman's knee. "I doubt Ramirov would have an apartment in a place where he has committed assassinations in the past. The Duchess of Windsor, Georges Pompidou, you name them. He *might* be staying with someone – in which case that person is dead, like that poor bastard in Hydra. It will be much easier for him to just stay in an hotel. Save all the hassle. He doesn't want to kill unnecessarily or draw attention to himself. He'll just use one of his many aliases – Hold on. Shit!" Melanie slapped herself on the forehead.

"What?" Christina frowned.

"Are we dumb cows or what? He won't be a foreigner checking in, will he? He will be a national, a Frenchman! We've asked Barking Dog to look for the wrong thing! We simply want all hotel check-ins."

"All hotel check-ins?" queried Christina. "For every hotel in Paris? For forty-eight hours? In August?"

"Yep," said Melanie, reaching for the keyboard.

"And how long will that take?"

"Several hours. If we want details of all of them. But let's pander to his ego again. Remember he's been using the IR initials. It will take Barking Dog a while to access the systems of every hotel in Paris, but let's refine our search to just one thing: his initials. Should take no time."

"No time?"

"Well, an hour or two maybe. Fancy going downstairs for a bit of a pamper meantime? The Health Centre looked empty when we came in..."

16:45 Place Vendôme

The Fayed party arrived at The Ritz Hotel having spent half an hour over at the house by the Bois de Boulogne. Diana had been impressed at the restoration of the house carried out under the supervision of Dodi's father.

While Henri Paul supervised the unloading of the luggage, Diana and Dodi went up to the hotel's Imperial Suite to relax for a couple of hours.

Outside, in the Place Vendôme, more paparazzi began to arrive: on foot, by car, by motorbike...

Sitting on her bike on the other side of the Place, Claudette watched the group of photographers grow and grow, like a swarm of bees attending their queen in the hive.

She hmmphed at her own simile. Sorry Lady Di, but the Brits had decreed that a Queen you were never to bee. She laughed. Her wit was as sharp as ever. But what about her skills? Somehow she had to get to Diana and both warn her of the imminent attempt on her life *and* get her to reveal the British secret.

Her Press ID would get her up to The Ritz doors, but no further. She could go in with her police authority, but would they accept it without checking? And if they checked, that would give away her whereabouts. Had Jamo put out a *Stop and Detain* on her?

This would take all her skill. She would make her move when the time was right.

Of one thing she was certain. Diana knew the secret for which her father had been killed. Tonight that secret would be revealed to Claudette Gerard.

18:30 Rue de Berri

At the same time as Dodi Fayed popped out from The Ritz to visit Alberto Repossi's Paris branch of his jewellery business just down on the Place Vendôme (concerning the ring from the 'Tell Me Yes' range that he had ordered for Diana), Christina Cascianis and Melanie Nathanson returned to their room at the Hotel California.

Christina had enjoyed an ayurvedic massage and Melanie had enjoyed a little private indulgence: colonic irrigation. Both women, of course, had had manicures and pedicures.

Melanie went across and opened the laptop. The screen immediately sprung into life. "Okay baby, show me what you've got." Melanie wiggled her hands.

Christina looked over the Englishwoman's shoulder.

Barking Dog's report read: **1 MATCH FOUND.**

"Yes!" Melanie snapped her fingers. "Ready for this?"

"Go for it." Christina was smiling in triumph.

Melanie pressed the Enter key.

19:00 Rue Cambon

The Ritz hotel's acting Director of Security, Henri Paul, watched as Dodi and Diana were driven away from the back entrance of the hotel in Rue Cambon. He knew that they were on their way back to Dodi's apartment at 1 Rue Arsène Houssaye, and that they intended to go out to dinner at *Le Benôit* near the Pompidou Centre.

Well, good luck to them. By using the back exit of the hotel they had avoided the paparazzi out the front, but word would soon spread.

Henri Paul was happy. Everything had gone well. Perhaps this would help confirm his post as Director.

Now he could go home for the night.

His hand touched the small business card in his jacket pocket. He had forgotten about it. Mr Jones's friend. He'd better call him. The British paid him well for his services, a hundred thousand francs a year, and he'd best not disappoint them.

20:00 Rue Arsène Houssaye

The Rue Arsène Houssaye is at the top end of the Champs Elysées, on the northern side. Dodi's apartment was on the top floor of Number 1.

At 20:00, amid a scuffle of security guards and photographers, the couple left the building for the short ride round into the Champs and down to *Sephora*, the classy perfume and make-up emporium.

By the time the Mercedes pulled up outside the shop, having been delayed by the traffic lights up at the Arc de Triomphe, a crowd had gathered, tipped off by the presence of the photographers that 'Someone' was arriving.

It was impossible for the couple even to get out of the car. Dodi said something to the driver and they moved off into the Saturday evening traffic on a circular route back to the apartment.

It happened very quickly, but Diana knew she had heard it.

The Mercedes pulled up back at 1 Rue Arsène Houssaye. The security men were pushing back a group of snapping photographers, and they were helped by Dodi's security man who leapt from the front passenger seat.

It was aural mayhem as the couple dashed the few metres from the car to the sanctuary of the building. The clicking of shutters, like some constant whirring machine, the shouts of the photographers' male voices, "Diana!", "Dodi!", "This way!", "Diana!".

Then she heard it. It was almost drowned by the male voices, but because it was a distinctly female voice it stood out. "Lady Di! I must talk with you! You are in danger!"

Diana looked around, but the security men had her and she was bustled inside the building.

21:15 Rue de Malte

The small bar in Rue de Malte off the Place de la République in east central Paris was off the tourist track and was frequented only by locals. This suited the Englishman fine, although one or two heads did turn when he ordered his beer and *croque monsieur* in good but accented French.

John Smith chose a small round table away from the bar and sat facing the front window.

He had just finished his *croque* when he saw an Austin Cooper pull up across the street. The man who got out was 41 years old, compact, balding, wearing glasses. He was dressed in a dark suit with a lighter shirt and tie. Smith recognised him from the file pictures: Henri Paul, acting Director of Security for The Ritz Hotel and MI6 informant (and doubtless informant for many other agencies as well).

Paul entered the bar and Smith stood up and waved him over.

"Mr Smith?"

"Mr Paul." They shook hands.

"Let me get you something," offered Smith.

Paul looked down at the half empty beer glass. "I will have one of those, thank you." His English was flawless. He sat down as Smith went over to the bar.

Two minutes later Smith was back with two beers and a bowl

of garlic croutons. "Would you like something more substantial to eat?"

"No, no, I eat well at work." Paul sipped his beer. "What can I do for you, Mr Smith? Mr Jones sent you?"

"Mr Jones gave me your name," explained Smith. "But he did not send me. I am here on behalf of someone else. Someone with a problem."

"Problems can always be solved, m'sieur."

"Quite. But this problem is very delicate. That's why we're calling on your services. We need someone who can use the utmost discretion." He had read in the file that Henri Paul conducted himself with a certain hubris, a *parvenu* aware of the heights to which he had risen. Smith was pandering to it.

Paul nodded. "What can I do for you?"

"My employer is having trouble with his ex-wife. Big trouble. He has asked that certain, er, solutions are found to his problem."

"Solutions?"

"Solutions."

"And this lady, she is a guest at the hotel?"

"Oh yes," said John Smith. "Oh yes."

21:45 Rue Arsène Houssaye

Dodi was the first out of the building in Rue Arsène Houssaye. He leapt through the held-open back door of the Mercedes. Diana followed. She was dressed in a black jacket, a black body, white trousers and sandals.

There was the usual clamour, the usual noise, the rushing river of clicking cameras, now flashing as the night descended.

But then she heard it again. The female voice. "Lady Di! What is the secret?"

This time Diana stopped by the car door and looked around, but all she could see was a mélange of faces, cameras, flashes, arms. People pushing and shoving each other, frantic to get *the* picture of her.

"Lady Di!"

Diana turned and looked over the top of the Mercedes. A red-helmeted figure was sitting on a motorbike next to the car. The visor was up and two big female eyes looked at her. "You are in danger!" The person shouted. "We must talk. There is something I want to know!"

A hand reached out from the back of the Mercedes and pulled Diana inside.

The car door slammed shut and the car sped quickly away towards the Avenue de Friedland.

21:50 Rue de Malte

"That is the most preposterous thing I have ever heard," said Henri Paul.

"Then you've led a very sheltered life," retorted John Smith.

"But *Princess Diana*?" There was disbelief in Paul's voice. "How can it be done?"

"That I leave up to you. Here," from an inside pocket of his jacket, Smith produced an envelope and slid it across the table. "A bonus of fifteen thousand, over and above your usual stipend. Not bad for a few moments' work."

"But what work! And I don't know how I can do it."

Smith put his hand into his other jacket pocket and brought out what looked like a small glass bottle, wrapped in a plastic bag. "Use this. We know it will be diluted, but it will still be effective. She will never know."

"This is unbelievable. What if she leaves the country? I hear they might be going back to England tomorrow."

"If they do, then we will see to it there. But they are equally likely to shoot off on one of their holidays again. And we want to get this matter determined and over with. And you never know, Henri," Smith reached across and slapped the Frenchman on his shoulder. "You might enjoy it!"

There was a ringing from inside Paul's jacket. He pulled out his chunky portable phone and had a conversation in rapid French.

After the call was finished, he nodded his head, looking across at John Smith. "It might be sooner than you think, m'sieur. That was the hotel. The couple are there, and they want me back."

"Good. I'll be staying at the Hotel Keppler, on Rue Keppler. You know it?"

"I can find it. The Sixteenth?"

"Yes. Let me know when it has been done."

Paul stood up, the envelope with the money already in his pocket, the plastic bag in his hand.

"And Henri," said Smith, retaining his grip on the Frenchman's hand after they had shaken. "Be discreet. Nobody is to know."

"No one will know, m'sieur. I guarantee it. They will never find out it was me."

Henri Paul turned and walked out of the bar.

21:55 Place Vendôme

The Mercedes arrived at the main entrance to The Ritz. More photographers were waiting here on the Place Vendôme, and those who had followed the couple were fast arriving on their motorbikes and in their cars.

The entire security team of The Ritz, less the Director, formed a passage for the couple.

There was the usual shouting, clicking and shoving. As they walked towards the hotel, Dodi smiled, seeming to like the attention. Diana was casting her eyes over the mêlée, seemingly looking for someone.

They walked through the revolving doors.

Inside, up above them, the security cameras began to record history.

22:10 Rue Cambon

The Ducati M900 was parked just metres from the small service entrance of The Ritz in the three-metre wide Rue Cambon.

Claudette was certain Diana had heard her – she had even stopped at the sound of her voice – but the Princess had been dragged inside the car.

Now there was no time to lose.

She showed her police ID to the man just inside the door. "*Sûreté Nationale,*" she said. "I must speak with your Director of Security immediately."

22:15 The Ritz Hotel

Dodi and Diana had intended to dine in the hotel's two-star *L'Espadon* restaurant, but because of the media frenzy outside and the staring heads inside, they decided to take their meal in the sitting room of their suite. The first course of scrambled eggs with mushrooms and asparagus was finished.

The second course of fish with vegetables tempura was being served (sole for Diana, turbot for Dodi) when Henri Paul rushed in.

"Sir, madame, excuse me."

"What is it, Henri?" Dodi did not looked pleased at the interruption. In the next hour he was going to propose to the mother of the future King of England, for God's sake!

"I'm sorry, sir. It's the police. Asking to speak to madame urgently."

"*What?* Oh for God's sake! Tell him to go away, we are eating."

"Yes, sir. And it is a 'her', sir. It's a police woman."

Diana looked up. "Is she on a motorbike?"

"Madame?"

"The policewoman."

Henri frowned. "Well, I presume she must be. She is dressed in leather."

"Tell her to wait. I will see her when we're finished.

22:59 The Ritz Hotel

Champagne (*Cristal*) was delivered to the Imperial Suite at 22:59. It was followed closely by Claudette, accompanied by Henri Paul.

"Inspector Ibrahim, madame," introduced Paul.

Claudette came over, only subconsciously registering the impressive high ceilings of the suite and the painted bas-reliefs on the walls. She took Diana's proffered right hand. "Your majesty." She looked at Dodi but no hand was offered.

Diana suppressed a giggle. "Call me Diana. It was you, wasn't it?"

"Me?"

"Out in the street."

"Yes, your – Yes. I must talk with you. It is – "

There was a bang and Claudette spun round, reaching inside her leather jacket.

Dodi had opened a bottle of champagne. He smiled. "You're good, Inspector. Sharp reflexes." He nodded. "Ever think of joining the private sector? My father pays handsomely." Was he being sarcastic?

"I might well need to, m'sieur." She turned back to Diana.

"And if that was a gun you were about to draw, you – Henri – are in trouble," sneered Dodi.

Paul did not react. He was used to Dodi's 'little ways'.

"Madame – Diana," said Claudette. "You are in danger. Can I speak freely?" Her eyes moved towards Paul and quickly back again.

"Please speak freely," said Diana. "Henri is a loyal and trusted friend."

"I have reason to believe that your life is under threat, madame."

"Are you sure? There are always nutters out there."

"It is more than that, madame. I have it on the utmost authority that an attempt will be made on your life while you are here."

"That is ludicrous," said Dodi. "Who by?"

"The British."

"The *British*? Oh come on, Inspector," sneered Dodi. " Do you really think the British would kill their own Princess?"

"It's Charles, isn't it?" said Diana thoughtfully.

"I don't know. But I have reason to believe there is an assassin out there."

Henri Paul walked over to the tall windows and looked down at the Place Vendôme. It looked like a crowd outside a Stage Door after a concert, waiting for the Superstar to appear. "Nothing will happen on my watch, I promise you," he sniffed.

He turned back around – and found Claudette pointing a gun at Diana's head.

23:00 Rue de Berri

In the Hotel California, Christina Cascianis and Melanie Nathanson were dressing up for a night on the town. At least, that is what it would look like. That was the alibi.

"You are sure it will happen tonight?" Christina was strapping a back-up Beretta and holster to the inside of her left thigh.

"He's here," reasoned Melanie. "Deaths on yachts never look natural – even if they are. Deaths in big cities – a dime a dozen."

"And we are just going to let him do it?"

"Grates, doesn't it?" Melanie was applying brown eye shadow (*Brun Aztèque* by Bourjois). "But Tel Aviv has pointed out that Ramirov is our mission, not Diana. The game must be played out."

"But could we not just stack the deck in her favour...?" wondered Christina.

They both looked at the laptop, thinking of the other information supplied by Barking Dog.

"Should we?" wondered Melanie.

"Letz," said Christina.

23:00 Rue Vavin

Pierre Jamo entered his apartment in Montparnasse and pulled off his clothes. They reeked of death and vomit.

Seven hours! He moaned to himself. Seven fucking hours the *Police Judiciaire* had detained him. And he had been the one who had found the body, the one who had called in the death! They treated him as if he were the murderer.

He had gone over his story again and again, with God knows how many people. He had an important meeting arranged with the Commissaire last night. (What about? That was BCP business, politically-sensitive, 'need to know'.) He had gone round to her apartment but had received no reply. She must have forgotten.

She did not turn up for work today. (A Commissaire working on a Saturday? Commissaire Colet often did. She was a very conscientious Commissioner.) So he went round to her apartment. Again there was no reply to his knock. But he could smell something. So he broke the door in. (He always carried the crowbar in his car.) Found her. Called the PJ.

That was his story.

And seven hours later they let him go home.

As pissed as sin, he turned the television on and went into the bathroom.

Ten minutes later, hair dripping, stark naked and with a towel in his hand, he stood motionless in front of the television.

The news bulletin was reporting Princess Diana's arrival in Paris that afternoon.

23:00 République

John Smith had stayed in the bar for an hour after Henri Paul had left, enjoying another three beers and chatting with the locals in his perfect but accented French. Now he walked north on the Rue de Malte and then turned west onto the Rue de Faubourg du Temple. He was satisfied. Job done. He had every faith in Henri Paul, fifteen thousand francs worth of faith, plus the one hundred thousand retainer Paul received each year from the British Security Services.

It was eleven o'clock on a Saturday night in Paris in August. Smith thought he might head up to Pigalle to celebrate – but then what if Paul succeeded sooner rather than later? He'd best return to the Hotel Keppler and wait.

He entered the Place de la République and trotted over to the metro. The musty popcorn smell of the subway system hit him as soon as he walked down the steps.

As he was on the *Ligne 9* train heading west, *Direction Pont de Sèvres*, he thought back to his meeting with Charles and Camilla two weeks previously.

"What do royals always do?" Camilla had asked.

They all knew the answer. The royals dithered, but then in the end they solved their problems.

There were conflicting reports about Diana's pregnancy. Her friend, Rosa Monckton, had reported that Diana had had her period when she was on holiday with her in Greece earlier in the month. If that was true, Diana could not be pregnant now.

But in contradiction, the US National Security Agency via their base at Menwith Hill in the north of England had listened to Diana telling another girlfriend on the phone that she was pregnant with Dodi's child [the Americans were monitoring Diana because of her anti-landmine campaign and activities, which would threaten US defence industry interests].

So The Boss had ordered Smith to determine Diana's pregnancy status for certain. If she was pregnant, she would be 'persuaded' to abort the child – or it would live in a social 'iron mask' for the whole of its life, denied and rejected by the establishment, a lifetime Fayed lie. But that was a bridge that would be crossed only if necessary.

John Smith had asked Henri Paul to obtain a sample of Diana's urine. A simple plumbing problem in the hotel, a failure to flush, don't worry madame, Henri will see to it – and that was it. If the urine tests were inconclusive, she would be sedated via a meal or a drink and be examined by a tame doctor. She would wake up none the wiser, with just a slight feeling of a hangover.

And that was the only involvement of His Royal Highness Prince Charles Philip Arthur George, Prince of Wales, Knight of the Garter, Knight of the Thistle, Knight Grand Cross of the Order of the Bath, Knight of the Order of Australia, Companion of the Queen's Service Order, Privy Counsellor, Aide-de-Camp, Earl of Chester, Duke of Cornwall, Duke of Rothesay, Earl of Carrick, Baron of Renfrew, Lord of the Isles, Prince Great Steward of Scotland and eldest son of Queen Elizabeth II, in the events of August 30 and 31 1997.

23:00 The Ritz Hotel

"So much for your security," said Claudette. "Mr Fayed was

right. A simple ID was all it took to get me in here." She put the gun back in its shoulder holster under her jacket. "It's just as well I am a policeman."

Diana sat there graciously. Henri Paul stood there open-mouthed. Dodi's first reaction of fear had turned to bravado. "Oh, you are going to work for us, madame," he nodded. "We have a vacancy at Director of Security level." He looked pointedly at Paul. He had taken a breath to say something else when his cell phone rang. It was on the mantelpiece. He went over, picked it up and frowned. "I'll take this in the other room. *Henri, allons.* I'll be back in a minute, darling."

The sitting room door closed behind them,

"So what should I do?" asked Diana.

Claudette turned round from watching the men leave. "Diana, what is the secret?" she asked abruptly.

Diana was confused. "What's the *what?*"

"The secret. The secret everyone dies for. I must know it. My father was killed because of it."

"I don't know what you mean - "

"We haven't much time. Many years ago. That is why the British are going to kill you now. The royal secret. Please, I beg you."

"I don't know any - " Diana stopped. She looked at the Frenchwoman in front of her. There was pleading in Claudette's eyes. Desperation. Oh my God – a royal secret. She never thought it was real.

Her mind went back eleven years to that Christmas at Sandringham, her row with Charles (perm any year from eleven for that one), the solace she had sought with grandma, the Queen Mother.

But surely the old woman had been drunk? Surely she had been kidding?

"I... I never thought she meant it," Diana said hesitantly. "Are you sure? I never thought it was true. She told me about the deaths... Oh my God. Is *she* going to kill me? Is it her? Why?

Why now?"

"What is the secret, madame? Please tell me."

"Inspector, it is not *a* secret," said Diana. "It is three secrets. Two in the past, one in the future. Each one building on the other. I don't think I should tell you..."

Claudette was a muscle-twitch away from re-drawing her gun. Then Diana said, "Oh, what the hell. Perhaps it is safer you do know. The more the merrier. The more the safer. They can't... kill us all..." She sounded uncertain. "The first secret is well-known. Wallis Simpson was a patsy. A cover-up for the affair of the century. David Windsor did not love her, she was the arranged bride to get him out of the country. It was the only reason he could abdicate. He would have to go if he intended to marry a divorcee. He could never be King. How ironic compared to today!" She paused briefly with her thoughts. Then she went on. "Because if he became King and was married to the barren Wallis, or indeed to anybody, his already-born daughter would never accede to the throne. But she did, and she's there to this day. The royal bloodline is pure. David Saxe-Coburg-Gotha, also known as David Windsor, and Elizabeth Bowes-Lyon. A love affair that lasted until his death. And their daughter Elizabeth."

Claudette said nothing, but her hand was shaking slightly.

Diana continued. "The second secret is an agreement. David Saxe-Coburg-Gotha was very proud of his German ancestry, his German blood. With the Teutonic English royal bloodline secure and his daughter destined to be Monarch, it was agreed that Germany would capitulate in 1945 – the war could have gone on for years, the German army was mighty. Do you really think the small little island of Britain was any match for them? But there is more than one way to win a war. The Germans had done what Britain wanted – annihilated over six million troublesome Jews. Before that, Zionism was a force in both countries – the Jews would have taken over the world. Has it never occurred to anybody that *Britain and Germany were effectively on the same side?* They wanted the same end-game. So did the Americans. They all wanted to make the world a better place – and they thought getting rid of the Jewish threat would do that. The fools."

She looked up at the Frenchwoman. "Hitler's assassination by his mistress was not in their plans. But the French, Yanks and Brits did not mind – he was a troublesome little runt. The plan was working. Britain's ruling family was, and remains to this day, German. Its bloodline is pure. And who really won the war? Who rules Europe today? Not France, not Britain. Fatso in Berlin, that's who rules Europe today.

"The third secret is the last part of the plan, very soon - "

The door opened and Dodi walked in.

"Can you believe it?" shouted Dodi. "Can you fucking believe it!"

Diana grimaced. She hoped he wouldn't swear like that in front of The Boys. Claudette turned to look at him.

"Do you know who that phone call was from? Fucking Israeli Intelligence. Israeli Intelligence! Some daft Jewish cow informing me that an attempt was to be made on your life tonight! Can you *believe* these people! The arrogance of them! And how did they get my number?"

Diana stood up. "What did you say to them?"

"Told them to mind their own fucking business. They even told me the man's name. A professional hit man, named Ramir something or other."

Claudette snapped back towards Diana. "Get away from the window now."

Diana ran over.

"Two independent confirmed sources," explained Claudette. She looked around. "Where is your security man?"

"He's ordering his staff to clear the Square in front of the hotel," said Dodi. "Onlookers are being sent back to the arcade on the other side. The Press can stay at a fifty metre perimeter –

but he is checking all their IDs and noting their names."

"So you believe the Israelis then?"

"I believed *you*. Fucking Jews."

"You need to leave here," advised Claudette.

"What do you mean? We're safe here," argued Dodi.

"In a huge hotel? Anyone could get in. You need to be somewhere smaller."

"Listen to her, Dodi," advised Diana.

"Where do you think we should go?" he asked, and then answered his own question. "Ah, I know!"

"This is what we'll do," said Claudette.

PART FIVE

Ω

FULFILMENT

Ω

Sunday August 31 1997

Paris, France

00:05 The Ritz Hotel

Henri Paul returned to the Imperial Suite with a sheet of paper in his hand. "I have checked all their IDs and listed their names. They are all genuine press photographers."

"Let me see," Claudette took the paper from him. She read the list of twenty names. There was Christian Martinez, Romauld Rat, Stephane Darmon, Claude Dumoulin, Jacques Langevin, Laslo Veres, Fabrice Chassery, David Oderkerken and Serge Benamou amongst others. No Ramir – something. Well, there wouldn't be, would there?

"So it is agreed," Claudette folded the paper and put it in her pocket. "They'll be expecting you to go to the Rue Arsène Houssaye. That will be the decoy. The full car and back-up, full security, usual drivers – but you will not be in it. Also they'll be expecting you to go out the front. We mustn't disappoint them. Henri, go and tell them we'll be leaving soon. Dodi, call your bodyguards."

00:10 Place Vendôme

Diana and Dodi left the Imperial Suite, and the bodyguards and others followed. Downstairs, the Mercedes 660 and the Range Rover pulled up at the front of The Ritz. There was a mass movement and shuffling from the crowd waiting outside.

00:18 The Ritz Hotel

As the Mercedes 660 and Range Rover pulled away from the hotel, some paparazzi followed on motorbikes. At the same time Diana and Dodi waited in the small lobby at the back of the hotel. Dodi had his arm touching Diana's back. Outside Henri Paul pulled up in the black Mercedes 280S, licence number 668 LTV 75. He opened the car's doors and then came into the hotel.

After a few exchanged words, the group walked out the back of the hotel. Despite their best laid plan, there were seven photographers waiting outside, among them Jacques Langevin, Fabrice Chassery, Claude Dumoulin, Serge Arnal, Christian Martinez, Romauld Rat and his driver Stephan Darmon.

Henri Paul smiled at the photographers, almost challenging. *"Bravo, mes amis.* Tonight you won't catch us."

Trevor Rees-Jones climbed into the front of the Mercedes, Dodi and Diana climbed into the back.

Nobody took any notice of the female who left the hotel immediately after them. She went over to her Ducati M900 motorbike next to the wall and put on her red crash helmet.

At the same time at the northern end of the Rue Cambon, Pierre Jamo turned his Fiat Uno a sharp right from the Boulevard de la Madelaine...

00:20 Rue Cambon

The Mercedes pulled away from The Ritz hotel and headed south on Rue Cambon. Two or three of the photographers decided to follow. The others picked up their portable phones to call their colleagues.

One bike in particular was keen to keep up with the Mercedes…

Pierre Jamo squinted down the narrow Rue Cambon and saw the flashguns going off outside the back of The Ritz. He saw the Mercedes pull away, and a few motorbikes take off after it. One of them seemed very keen. It was a big bike, like a Ducati.

That was Claudette's bike.

Claudette Ibrahim watched Diana and Dodi go. She wished them well. Her job was done.

Diana had told her the Windsor Secret. It was shocking. The world had been fooled. Millions had died unnecessarily. But worst of all was the third part, the part that was to come early in the next century. Would they really attack New York?

What should she do with the knowledge? One thing was for certain, she was in danger. Mortal danger. If the Brits knew she knew…

She was looking south down the Rue Cambon as a white Fiat Uno shot past her. The car hardly registered with her. She was thinking about Lady Diana.

The Brits were going to kill one of their own – at least they were going to try to. But the decoy car plan should work. If not, the decoy destination should work, at least until the men from Harrods in London could get to the Press and blow the assassination plot wide open.

As for her, she needed to disappear. She had avenged her father, she had been told the secret. Time to start anew somewhere.

She fingered the piece of paper in her pocket, the one Diana had given her as they waited to leave the hotel. It was Diana's direct line telephone at her home in Kensington Palace, London. "Ring me," Diana had said. "If there is anything you want me to do for you. Ever. Ring me."

Claudette Ibrahim smiled and turned the ignition on the Ducati.

00:22 En route

The Mercedes turned right into the Rue de Rivoli. In his wing mirror, Henri Paul could see a few motorbikes behind the car. One seemed to be ahead of the others. There was also a white Fiat.

They passed into the Place de la Concorde and turned left with the traffic flow.

Paul smiled to himself. This is where they would be expecting him to turn right into the Champs Elysées. He put on his right indicator and then pressed his foot down on the accelerator.

The Mercedes shot straight ahead across the bottom of the Champs, heading towards the Seine.

In his mirror Paul saw two bikes actually turn into the Champs, but the closest bike stuck with him. As did the Fiat.

Pierre Jamo cursed. It was not Claudette, it was not even a Ducati, it was a BMW. He had gotten close enough to see that the helmeted, leather-clad rider was far too tall and chunky to be her. It was probably just another dumb paparazzo.

He would just get up close to the Merc to make sure everyone was all right inside and then he would go home. He really couldn't think straight anymore. He needed sleep.

Ω

The convoy of the Mercedes, the Fiat and the motorbike passed into the Cours la Reine on the banks of the Seine. They were travelling at 70 kilometres per hour, ten kilometres above the speed limit of 60 kph but by no means speeding. They entered the first tunnel.

The Fiat accelerated on the inside of the Mercedes. Jamo could see four people inside. They seemed normal. The couple in the back were laughing.

The motorbike accelerated on the outside.

They came out of the tunnel just underneath the southern end of the Avenue Franklin D Roosevelt.

In the Mercedes, Henri Paul was pleased with himself. The plan was working. Their destination was not Dodi's flat in the Rue Arsène Houssaye but the other Fayed property, 24 Boulevard Suchet, the 'Villa Windsor'. He would take a right up the slip-road before the Alma Tunnel. Then it was a straight route: Avenue Georges Mandel, Avenue Henri Martin, Boulevard Suchet. Simple.

The motorbike overtook him on the left.

Paul began to cruise to the right towards the slip-road, but he wrenched the steering wheel back as he saw a Fiat up by the side of him. There was a faint knock and a scrape as the vehicles touched.

It was too late to get to the slip road now, he would have to go down through the Alma Tunnel.

There was a thump and he saw something round on the windscreen.

In the back, the laughing Diana looked up at the beautiful lights on the Eiffel Tower across the river as they descended into the tunnel.

00:30 Alma Tunnel

On the BMW, Ian Ramsey pulled up level with the front wheels of the Mercedes. Steering the bike with his left hand, he reached down into a bag attached on the fuel tank between his legs and brought out what looked like the bottom of a large tin of shaving soap. It was a *Stunpet* – a combination stun grenade and limpet mine which would stick to any surface.

Ramsey turned his arm around and slammed the *Stunpet* on the windscreen of the car. Then he accelerated down into the Alma Tunnel, way ahead of the Mercedes now.

He began to slow as a Citroen and a couple of other cars passed, and then he pulled a small device out of his top pocket and pressed it.

The Mercedes entered the tunnel only 20 kph above the tunnel speed limit of 50.

Henri Paul only had time to register the round object stuck onto the windscreen. Then it simultaneously flashed and exploded. The flash had the brightness of seven suns and it instantly blinded Paul. The percussive explosion blew out his ear drums.

Instead of curving left with the road in the tunnel, the Mercedes went straight, clipping the right wall and then flying across the carriageway, spinning into the thirteenth concrete support pillar with an almighty bang and crushing of metal. It then bounced back off the pillar and span again, coming to rest facing backwards down the tunnel, the way it had come.

Ramsey slid the BMW to a stop, turned the bike around and drove back to the wrecked vehicle. The horn on the car was stuck and blaring. Smoke was rising from the mangled engine.

Beneath the airbag, the driver was squashed to a pulp, one of his hands jutted through the broken windscreen. The front passenger was held rigid by his seat belt, the airbag pressing against him. Where his face should be was a cascade of blood.

Ramsey pulled open the back, off-side passenger door. Over the other side, Dodi Fayed was stretched out, his legs broken and bent at a terrible angle. His eyelids were open but his eyes had turned back in his head. He was dead.

Near to Ramsey, his target was doubled up between the front seat and the back seat, her head between the two front seats. She had a cut on her forehead and was disorientated, but otherwise she seemed unhurt. She looked at Ramsey. She said, "My God, my God."

Ramsey flipped open the pocket on his leather jacket and withdrew a small, three centimetre long, one centimetre wide aerosol, like a perfume sampler. He took the top off and, clinically, dispassionately, sprayed something into Diana's face. She was not even aware of it.

Ramsey replaced the top of the aerosol and put it back in his pocket. Then he pulled out a few sachets of heroin and threw them into the car. Cosmetics. He closed the car door back over, and walked off back towards his bike as paparazzo Romauld Rat arrived with his camera. The smoke was still billowing, and the car horn was blaring incessantly, noisily, eerily.

Ramsey was half hidden by the smoke by the time he reached his bike. He looked back at the Mercedes. The colourless, odourless, cyanide gas had served him and his previous masters well in the past, notably killing Dr Lev Rebet in 1952 and used by Ramirov himself on Georges Pompidou in 1974. Diana, Princess of Wales, would be dead within the hour.

He straddled his bike and looked back one last time. He said, "Welcome to history, bitch."

Then he sped off out of the Alma Tunnel.

PART SIX

Ω

END-GAME

01:00 Rue Vavin

Pierre Jamo felt the bump from the Mercedes as he took the slip road up onto the Cours Albert 1er, but he thought nothing of it. Bumps happen all the time in Paris.

Across the Pont de l'Alma, he took the Avenue Bosquet. The streets were reasonably quiet at that hour of the morning, and he was pulling into Rue Vavin by 01:00.

That hadn't been Claudette on the bike, and he was happy that Diana and Dodi were all right. He'd seen them laughing in the back of their car.

But what had happened to Claudette, he wondered? Both literally and figuratively. What had happened to turn his talented, feisty, clever, *sexy* Inspector into a serial killer? Or had she been conning him all along? Was this yet another woman who had led him a merry dance, who had fooled him?

And where was she now? He had been tempted to go back to her apartment one more time but, frankly, he was just so damned tired. He would leave her to her fate. He did not owe her anything.

But, he thought regretfully, she was a damn good screw. 'Was' being the operative word.

As he was locking his car, he noticed one of his back lights was smashed. Shit, the Mercedes must have bumped him harder than he thought. More expense!

Normally he would walk up to his apartment on the third floor, but having exercised his legs today first in Colet's block and then in Claudette's block, he decided to take the lift.

The elevator was the old but effective see-through variety, with double concertina gates, going up the middle of the stairwell. It hummed loudly as it crept upwards.

As the lift raised his head slowly above the second floor and his apartment door came into view, Jamo frowned. For a moment he wondered whether he was back in Montmartre and not Montparnasse, and this was Claudette's place. Because the door to his apartment looked just like hers had after he had kicked it in – the wood around the lock was splintered. And the door was open a few centimetres.

Before the lift had clunked to a stop, Jamo had his gun in his hand. What the hell was this? Was it her?

He peeked into his hallway without touching the door. His lights were on and blazing. Whoever it was, if they were still there they were announcing their presence.

His foot pushed the front door open. He was pleased it did not creak.

The salon door was ajar, and the lights were on inside. Gun raised, he pushed the door open.

The room was empty. But now he could hear a sound. Running water. And something else. A buzzing.

The kitchen was off the salon, and the bathroom was beyond, off the kitchen.

The kitchen door was open, lights on, nobody there. The bathroom door was closed. That's where the noises were coming from.

Jamo turned the door handle and the door moved. It was not locked. Finger lightly but determinedly on the trigger of his Glock 17, he opened the door. The sound of the running water and the buzzing noise got louder.

Looking in, his eyebrows rose.

The gun lowered.

Claudette was standing there.

She was completely naked and she was using his mains electric razor to smooth out the stubble on her already-shaven pudendum. Next to her, water was running into a foam-filled bath, steam rising.

She looked up as the door opened and smiled in delight. "Hi, Chief!"

"What," he asked slowly, "are you doing here?"

"I didn't know what time you'd be back. I was making

myself nice for you. Care to join me?" she nodded towards the bath. Turning the razor off, she rubbed between her legs. "Nice," she nodded. "Just as you like it."

"I have been looking for you," Jamo said carefully, cautiously checking the rest of the room with his eyes. "Lots of people have."

"I know. Now you've found me. But look, I'm unarmed as you can see, you can put the gun away." She came over to him and stroked the side of his face. As always, her pert, muscular, naked body was mesmerizing him. She took hold of the Glock and he released his grip. Carefully she put the gun down on the clothes basket.

"What are you up to?" he asked.

"I know I've got a lot of explaining to do," she pushed his jacket off his shoulders, and he could smell the warmth in her hair. She stood on tiptoe and lightly kissed his lips. "And I will, I will tell you everything. I will tell you why." Her lips were brushing against his as she spoke. "I have found out the secret." She pressed her lower body against his. "Ah, that's a better greeting for a lady. I know that's not your gun and I *know* you're pleased to see me."

Jamo felt her hands against his chest as she unbuttoned his shirt. He was rigid in his trousers, and thank God she started to touch him as she undid his belt.

"And I will tell you who I really am," she said.

"I know who you really are," he retorted as she pulled his trousers and underpants down and reached round and rubbed the hairy cheeks of his bottom. She was kneeling in front of him and his hard dick was banging against her face.

"Not today," she kissed his knob. "Today let's pretend I have another name." She rubbed him with her right hand, sucking on him. Then she looked up and said, "Call me Gillian." She moved away and stood up in one motion.

"Call you *what?*" Jamo was standing there erect, trousers and pants around his ankles, shoes and socks still on.

She giggled. "Gillian. She won't be using the name any more. Come, bathe with me." She beckoned with her finger.

"You little bitch." Jamo hopped across the room towards her, and she laughed out loud.

When he got within distance, she reached out, grabbed his penis firmly and used his own hopping momentum to push him into the bath. He went over the rim, bottom first, legs hanging over the side. Water splashed up and over onto the floor.

"Hey!" he shouted.

Gillian reached behind her and turned the razor back on. Jamo could see what was going to happen and he struggled to get out of the bath, but he was hampered by his tied feet.

She threw the razor into the bath.

It was as spectacular as she had expected. Cracks, crackles, smoke, Jamo jumping up and down, eyes nearly popping out of his head.

She did not turn the current off, it would probably blow eventually. She turned, and the last thing Pierre Jamo saw was her superb bottom walking away from him.

He did not live to see her turn back in the doorway, nor to hear her say, "You Parisians and your accidents in the bath. Will you never learn?"

Singing *Bordeaux Rosé* she went out and closed the bathroom door behind her.

01:15 Rue d'Italie

Ian Ramsey parked the BMW in the small Rue d'Italie down in the 13th, put the crash helmet on the seat and walked away.

It would be a long walk back to his hotel at Place de Clichy, but it had to be done. The authorities would have their hands full tonight but, if there were any eagle-eyed witnesses, they might – just *might* – be looking for an unaccounted for paparazzo on a BMW.

And he would not hail a cab. Someone on his own at this hour of the morning on this historic day, would be remembered. The night's events might even be on the radio already.

02:00 Rue Vavin

Claudette Gerard spent some time clearing all traces of herself from Pierre Jamo's apartment. No prints anywhere, no tell-tale girly items she might have inadvertently left behind.

After thirty minutes she went back into the bathroom just to ensure Pierre was dead. He was, well and truly. The bowels had vacated themselves into the bath, which was unfortunate – and smelly – but never mind, couldn't be helped. He had no housekeeper so, she realised, he might not be found for some while. Not until his absence from work was noticed. And who would notice that? She would not be there, and The Bitch Colet was dead. Old Sergeant Goise might start looking in about a week.

She laughed. Was she bothered?

04:00 Place de Clichy

Ian Ramsey reached the Hotel Mercure Montmartre at 04:00, having walked a circuitous route across the Boulevard de Port Royal (he saw a slowly moving ambulance and some police cars on the Boulevard, but he thought nothing of it)), past the Jardin du Luxembourg, across the river via the Île de la Cité and then along the various side streets up through the Bourse and St Lazare then straight up the Rue d'Amsterdam.

As he crossed the Place Clichy, he pulled out his cell phone and began to make a call.

With 305 rooms in the hotel, the front door and the Reception were always open. At this hiatus hour between night and early morning there were fewer people about, but he still walked over to the lifts unnoticed, talking softly on his cell phone. One or two late night travellers were returning (Paris on a Saturday night was still the place to be), and he had to share the lift with a couple of middle-aged women.

He used his phone conversation to ignore them and they ignored him as they travelled upwards, but the black haired woman burped as they passed the third floor and that started the red haired one giggling.

The lift reached the sixth floor, and Ramsey stepped out. He heard the lift doors close behind him.

"Yes, thank you," he said into the cell phone as he put his key card in his door. Then he was aware of running footsteps, muted on the carpet, coming towards him. He turned to find the two women who had been in the lift. They had identical Heckler & Koch P7 handguns with bulbous silencers, pointing at his head.

"Hello Ilich," said Christina Cascianis, pushing her gun against the back of his head and forcing him into the room. "Remember me?"

"There must be some mistake - " He lowered his hand holding the phone.

"None at all," said Christina as Melanie closed the door. "Not this time."

Christina shot him in the head from behind. The bullet went through the skull and took out his left eye, which was later found under the minibar. Christina stood over the body and emptied all thirteen of the 9mm Parabellum cartridges into his head, the body jumping with each one.

"Not this time," she repeated.

She spat onto the corpse. "For Stelios."

04:30 Rue Larmarck

The Ducati motorbike roared up the quiet backstreets of Montmartre and stopped at the end of Rue Lamarck. Claudette Gerard wondered whether Will The Cat had returned. She hoped so. She must leave Paris now and she wanted her baby for company.

She reached the top floor and thought of Jamo as she saw her broken front door. *Bastard.*

She went in and pushed the door closed behind her.

Then she heard a noise. In the *salle de jour*. Yes! She smiled. She had left the window open and Will was home.

She pushed open the door, and there was the cat waiting for her. She bent down and Will jumped into her arms. "Hello, baby."

"Hello," said a female voice.

Claudette's head shot up.

"Come away from the door." Over by the window was a small, elegant woman dressed in denim jeans and loose white silk shirt. Her dark hair fell down either side of her face, but it could not hide the large surgical dressing on the left side of her neck. She was holding a Smith and Wesson.

Oh, merde.

"Remember me?" asked Gisele Joudeh.

"Of course," Claudette stood up slowly. "You are Becker's girlfriend. I thought you were dead. Silly me. I am sorry I did not finish the job." Claudette kept her eyes on the other woman but mentally she was looking around the room. She was hampered by the cat in her arms.

"You are quite the charmer, aren't you" said the Lebanese. "Why did you hurt Ron?"

"I didn't, you did."

"You were torturing him, weren't you?"

Claudette frowned tightened her grip on the cat.

"What did Ron say to you?" Gisele saw the grip tighten. "And please, don't make me shoot your cat, she is not involved in this."

"In what?"

"Do you know the expression 'honey trap'? The Brits were involved in something. Courtesy of Ron, I had learnt of their plans. I heard him talking to you about Diana."

"I just needed to know why my father died."

"Your father? What has that got to do with the death of Diana?" Gisele was surprised.

"The death?" Claudette was perplexed. "What do you mean death?"

"She was killed tonight."

Claudette shook her head. "She can't have been. I was…" She thought back to Diana and Dodi driving off in the Mercedes. How could Diana be dead?

She looked at Gisele and her eyes went blank. Stone-faced, she lowered her arms and the cat jumped down. In her right hand Claudette was holding her gun.

"Put it down," ordered Gisele.

"Fuck you." Claudette raised her arm.

Both women fired.

Gisele jumped to her right as she pulled the trigger, and Claudette's bullet thudded into the chair behind her.

Claudette did not move. She grinned at the Lebanese woman prostrate on the floor and she was on the verge of laughing. Then the hole in the centre of Claudette's forehead popped out a clot of blood and the crimson river rolled down between her eyes. She crumpled to the floor.

After a moment, the other woman slowly stood up. She brushed fluff and cat hair off of her denim jeans. She looked at the body on the floor and then gave it a tentative kick. Nothing except a twitching left foot. The Frenchwoman was dead.

Well, what was all that about? she wondered. Had it anything to do with her mission?

Gisele Joudeh, a member of the Lebanese Department of General Security, gave a final look around the room, and left.

On the floor next to Claudette, Will The Cat rubbed her nose against her mistress.

"Weow," she said.

Ω

Saturday August 30 1997

Sarasota, Florida, USA

In the USA it was still Saturday. It was 23:00 local time when the death of Diana, Princess of Wales, was confirmed on the networks. A tragic accident, cause by the picture-hungry paparazzi.

He nodded in satisfaction, turned the volume off on his TV and walked out onto the lanai.

The evening was hot but the humidity of the day had evaporated. He eased himself into his hot tub, alone this time.

Ilich Ramirov leant his head back on the marble edge and closed his eyes. He couldn't help but smile.

He had heard Ian Ramsey's execution on the cell phone – and he had heard who had done it. The Israelis. The damn, fucking Israelis. But his smile was one of "I knew it."

Ever since the stupid French had announced the death of Ilych Ramirez Sanchez – and had then hastily withdrawn the announcement – he knew the Jews would be after him. He had been left in peace for the three years they thought he had been incarcerated, but now they were onto him.

Well, damn them. They did not know that in those three years, he had created a brand. He had recruited the cream of the world's professional assassins and mercenaries, from the US, from Scotland, Ireland, Russia, Mexico and, yes, even Israel. A co-operative of callous, emotionless, highly skilled killing machines who would terminate anyone – for the right money.

Like 'Best Western' was not one hotel chain but a group of independent hotels, like 'Wimpy' was not one restaurant chain but a group of franchises, like 'James Patterson' was no longer one author but a group of co-writing authors, so 'Ilich Ramirov' was no longer one assassin but a group of assassins.

And did the pathetic Israelis really think that he would go on an assignment *and use his own initials?* The unfortunate 'Ian Ramsey' was his patsy, his stoolpigeon. Ramsey had served him well. He had completed his mission and he had lured the Israelis. Ramirov hoped Ramsey's heirs, whoever they may be, enjoyed the five million US dollars Ramirov had paid him.

As the warm water lapped against his chest, Ramirov felt a longing. His wished the whore Candice was with him. He needed a tangible celebration. To celebrate on your own was not to celebrate at all. And anyway, it would make him go blind – and he only had one eye left!

He reached for his bottle of *Coors* on the ceramic edge of the tub.

Now the Israelis really thought he was dead. That was good, and he wished he could leave it at that. But there was an old saying: once is happenstance, twice is coincidence, three times is enemy action.

The meddlesome Greek Christina Cascianis. Cyprus 1974. Khartoum 1994. Paris 1997.

Three times.

Enemy action.

He began to formulate his plans.

Ω

Sunday August 31 1997

Balmoral, Scotland

"Mummy," said Elizabeth, Queen of England. "Mummy, I'm sorry to disturb you but something dreadful has happened."

The ninety-seven year old matriarch of the British Royal Family slowly opened her eyes from the pretence of sleep. "Mm? Elizabeth? What is it?" She wished she was at Birkhall instead of the main house, but her cottage was being redecorated. So she had to go through with it.

"It is positively awful, Mummy. Diana has been killed. In a car crash. In Paris."

The old woman looked at her daughter, her beautiful pure blood Elizabeth.

So, it was over. The last person to know the secret had been expunged. It was a pity it had to be Diana, but it had to be done. And it wasn't as if she was a member of the family any more. Or royal. She was simply the carrier of the bloodline of the family. Provided William survived, the line would be pure. Henry would never be King, for obvious reasons.

What she had done, what she had had to do, would never be known. The secret was dead.

She pulled herself up in her bed and held her arms out. "Oh my darling," she said. "That is dreadful. Come, kiss Mummy."

Clarence House, London, England

Sir Kenneth Dean, Senior Secretary to Her Majesty Queen Elizabeth the Queen Mother, gently replaced the telephone on its receiver. Her Majesty had called to thank him for his speed and efficiency – and, of course, for his discretion. His promised reward would be forthcoming.

Dean sat back in his chair behind his desk in his small, austere office in the Queen Mother's London residence. He thought back over the years. Back to 1979 when they had at last obtained the documents that had been retained for over thirty years by Wallis Simpson, Duchess of Windsor. Documents that had kept the Duchess alive for so many years. Documents that had then been stolen. Many had had to die to retrieve the documents and protect the secret.

At that time, he was plain Kenneth Dean, Under Consul at the British Embassy in Paris (the knighthood and secretarial position were six months away 'for services rendered'). The documents had been retrieved and he had visited Her Majesty at Clarence House and had given her the sealed envelope.

He had watched as Her Majesty tore the envelope and contents into small pieces and let them fall into a glass ashtray. She had then taken a cigarette lighter, lit the pile in three places, and stared as the paper charred and curled in on itself, reducing to ashes.

But she had not looked inside the envelope before burning it.

Now, eighteen years later, Sir Kenneth Dean unlocked the bottom left drawer of his desk and pulled out an A5 envelope. He lifted the flap and took out the contents. Carefully he laid it on his desk.

He looked at the old sepia envelope with the royal crest and the initials E.P on the back. It was about time, he thought, that he found out why so many people had had to die.

He picked up the envelope and took out the two pieces of

paper inside.

"It is absolutely black-and-white horrendous murder."
- Mohamed Al Fayed, 6 January 2004.

"There is not one drop of blood in my veins that is not German."
- David Saxe-Coburg-Gotha,
also known as David Windsor,
King Edward VIII of England.

Anyone who knows the secret, dies.

Now you do...

DAVID CULLEN

THE EYE OF
MAKARIOS

IN A WORLD OF TERROR THE ONLY TRUTH IS BETRAYAL

THE EYE OF MAKARIOS

David Cullen

1974. A world in turmoil. Terrorism is rife.

In the Middle East, *El Fateh* plan their first nuclear strike. The Irshman, their hardware supplier, wants a very special item in payment.

In the Mediterranean, Cyprus is an island about to be divided. Resistance leader Grivas is dying. He wants to hit his enemy from beyond the grave.

In Israel, the security services want to finish off their enemies once and for all.

In Europe, Sally wants to find her missing lover.

In a world about to implode, they all have one common link:

THE EYE OF MAKARIOS

ISBN: 978-0-9559911-0-3

Available from *amazon, Lulu* and other online booksellers and thru all good bookshops.

DAVID CULLEN

THE MESRINE CONCLUSION

ONLY ONE MAN CAN RETRIEVE THE SECRET - IF HE CAN STAY ALIVE

THE MESRINE CONCLUSION

David Cullen

1978. Only two people still alive know the explosive dark secret of the British Royal House of Windsor.

One lies in her dotage in France, the other continues to rule the royal household in Britain as she has done for 40 years.

A robbery in Paris. The secret is stolen. It must be found at all costs. Police enquiries draw a blank. They need help. There is only one man with the skills to locate the secret – Jacques Mesrine, France's Public Enemy Number One.

But there are those that want the secret for themselves and others who will stop at nothing to ensure the secret remains hidden.

Can Mesrine find the secret before the hunters find him? Death, treachery and double-cross all lead to

THE MESRINE CONCLUSION

ISBN: 978-0-9559911-1-0

Available from *amazon, Lulu* and other online booksellers and thru all good bookshops.

Lightning Source UK Ltd.
Milton Keynes UK
UKOW03f1808290414

230819UK00001B/88/P